Heather

By
Charlotte Wood

Charlotte Wood (signature)

Rotten Poetry

Published by Rotten Poetry
RottenPoetry.net

2024

Printed and bound in the UK

Paperback ISBN: 978-1-0686633-0-7
eBook ISBN: 978-1-0686633-1-4

Well drawing, cover design and layout by Darren Ellis

Heather and Fern icon by Emma Jane Bennett, ejbennett.co.uk

To Dad,
Who never doubted me for a second.

To Mr James Taylor;
My GCSE English Teacher,
To whom I promised to dedicate my first book.

Chapter One.

It was fantastic. Everything that she had wanted.

After spending her first year of university in a hall of residence with five other people she didn't know and, as it turned out, she didn't really like either, it was a great relief for Fern to be out on her own. She had decided to take a flat by herself. She had always preferred her own company and this was something that she had wanted for a long time. A chance to live by herself. No need to rely on other people.

The flat was small, but it had all the essentials. There was a kitchen just big enough for her to fit into. The walls were decorated with drab brown tiles that spoke volumes about the age of the place. It was small but it had everything that Fern needed to get by. An oven, a microwave, a sink and a fridge freezer questionably positioned so she had to squeeze past it to get to the door. There was no washing machine, there was barely enough room for what was in there already, but there was a laundrette just down the road. There was a bathroom; well it could be more accurately described as a shower room. The room was the wrong shape for a bath, so the landlord had settled for a shower. The living room only had an armchair and a television in it with a circular rug on the floor between. There was a tall thin book shelf set against one of the walls and a window looking out over the rear yard.

The wallpaper was old, it smelt musty if you got too close to it, which was all the time considering the size of the room. It was a faded shade of blue and had little periwinkles on it. Fern did not like it very much. It reminded her of the old people's home her grandmother had been forced to move into when she was unable to look after herself any more. But Fern didn't worry; she didn't suppose that the wallpaper of a rented flat mattered that much. The bedroom was a different story. It had originally been two rooms but the landlord had knocked it into one when he had realised that

7

it was impossible for more than one person to live here at the same time. He had also put mirrors along one of the walls which Fern thought odd. She hoped it had been a style choice and not because he was a creep.

The flat was on the first floor of a two storey building. Fern was no expert but it looked Victorian, like the rest of the houses on the street. There were a lot of old Victorian properties in the area, a throwback to industries long since forgotten. She supposed there were great stories to be told about this street, when it was once a booming industrial area. Those days had gone though, and it was now a string of less-than-great flats for students and low-income households, littered with betting shops and convenience stores.

Originally, the rooms upstairs had been the bedrooms and the rooms downstairs had been used for the cooking and a small study, that sort of thing. It had been converted in the 1970s to make it into two flats, no doubt so the owner could make money from the emerging student population. Fern had chosen this flat because of the rent. She had looked at other one-person flats that had been bigger and closer to the city centre but the rent had been too high for one person to manage on a student loan. This flat was ideal. The right price for one and the location was fine because she had a little car that her dad had been good enough to buy for her before she moved away.

So Fern moved in to her modest little flat, put a pizza in the oven and sat down to watch some TV. She was happy. She loved her parents, but she was glad they were two hundred miles south of her and unable to bail her out. She saw the independent life style as a challenge. If she forgot to lock the door or turn the oven off she would have no one to blame but herself. She thought about this as she nibbled her pizza and watched the television. She wasn't even aware of what she was watching because she was so deep in thought.

As the light faded behind her closed curtains she imagined what the next day would be like. It would be her first full day alone and she couldn't wait. She would get up early, have a shower and have breakfast. She couldn't function without a decent breakfast inside her so she always insisted on making time for a proper healthy meal. She considered this as she finished off the last slice of the greasy cheese pizza she had cooked as her first meal in the flat. She was a student after all. After her breakfast she planned on going for a walk round the area to acquaint herself with her surroundings. She has seen an entrance to a park on the way over and thought that might be a good place to start. As this thought went through her mind, her head lolled back onto the high back of the arm chair and she began to drift off. She had spent all afternoon unpacking and was exhausted. She had been so busy planning her day ahead in her mind she hadn't noticed that the TV had switched itself off. She fell asleep in the armchair and began to dream.

She was dressed in an Edwardian school uniform and was walking towards a door that appeared to be of giant proportions in relation to her size. It was made out of wood and had huge brass hinges the like of which she had only ever seen before on old churches and castles. The door creaked open as she approached revealing a dark room beyond. As she tried to see what was inside she seemed to drift inside through the darkness and into a dimly lit foyer. She turned left down a seemingly endless corridor. She went past classroom after classroom of female students dressed as she was, being taught by nuns. Was this a Catholic school? As she drifted past each classroom the nuns turned to look at her. As they saw her, their faces became contorted with horror, mouths opening to unnatural degrees and their eyes blackening, all colour drained from their cheeks. Fern didn't want to look at them but she couldn't help it. She felt uneasy and wanted to leave but she continued to move towards the end of the long corridor.

Fern counted eight classrooms before she reached the door at the end. She turned right this time, the door opened and she floated outside into a large field. This must be where they played at lunch time. This thought briefly went through Fern's mind as she saw where she was heading. She was travelling faster now; all Fern could see was what was directly in front of her. It appeared to be a well. It made sense at that time in history, she thought, as she stopped abruptly at the edge of the well. The well was made of stone, roughly cut into the shapes needed. There was a cast iron frame above which the chain and bucket were attached to. Moss grew between the gaps in the stones and the grass around the well had been beaten back by the feet of those using the well.

Fern was now in control of herself again and she looked around. Behind the well was a gentle slope that turned into a farmer's field. It had recently been ploughed and she could see gulls diving down to eat the creatures that had unwillingly been revealed to the world. Fern turned around and saw that all the pupils and the nuns had left their classrooms and were lined up outside. They were all staring at Fern. Some of the children were horrified by her and twisted their bodies away so they did not have to look and others were just looking, rather complacently at the girl at the well. There were some who were staring at Fern with fear in their faces but were unable to turn away. Fern turned around quickly. She leant on the wall of the well gasping for air. What were they so scared of? She was just like them! She was no different! Then she realised that the well was full. She leaned over to see her reflection in the water. The face looking back at her was that of a twelve year old girl. There was nothing unusual about it. A breeze blew and the water began to ripple. The image changed. Fern wanted to scream but was unable. The face was now pale in the cheeks and the lips were as black as the night. The face was sunk back so far the skin was clinging to the cheek bones. The mouth set open, as if she was gasping for air. Her gums had receded and turned black. Her teeth were rotten and cracked. And the eyes, the eyes disturbed Fern more than anything. They were bulging, wide open and staring back at her without registering what they were looking at. As Fern gazed into them she saw nothing. There was nothing inside, no mind alive with thought behind them. The eyes were dead.

Fern woke up with a start. Her plate with three pizza crusts left over fell to the floor. She was still in the armchair but it was now morning. She moved her stiffened body and glanced at her watch. It was already 9.30am She muttered a swear word and got up. As she rose she remembered the dream and sat back down. She had not suffered from nightmares since she was a child. She pulled herself together.

"It was just a dream. Just a stupid dream." She muttered to herself and got up to get on with her planned day.

Fern had arrived in her flat on Saturday; spent Sunday getting herself organised and started her second year of her English degree on Monday. Sunday had gone by as she had planned, and she was relieved when she woke up on Monday morning in her bed with the memory of a dream about an orange monkey called Zeph. She had a 9am lecture that morning on Chaucer and she enjoyed it. She took it as a sign of things to come and left the lecture theatre in a good mood. On the way out of the university building she was accosted by her Scottish friend from the first year, Erica.

"Hey Fern! Long time no see!"

"Hi Erica. How was your summer?"

"You really want to know?"

Fern nodded.

"I spent the entire three months stacking shelves in *Tesco*."

"Wow!" Fern offered sarcastically

"I did it to save up for a last minute deal on a holiday, but I got impatient and spent it on clothes instead. Do you like

11

my shoes?"

Fern looked down and saw Erica's clearly new, expensive trainers.

"They are lovely!" Fern lied.

"Thanks. Hey, do you fancy coming out with me tonight? I'm going to the union and I'd love some company."

Fern said she'd love to and they agreed to meet at the union at 10pm. It was well known to all second years that Monday night was the best night to go to the student union because no first years went.

Fern went to her seminar at 11am, listened to the tutor discuss women's literature for two hours, and went home. She had her lunch, read some of *The Canterbury Tales,* brushing the odd crumb from her sandwich off the pages as she did so, and started getting ready to go out. She left the house at 9.30, and got to the union just in time to meet Erica. When Fern arrived Erica was wearing white from head to toe. As someone who was prone to clumsiness, Fern never understood the appeal of white clothes.

They had a great night and Erica, as usual, went home with at least three phone numbers. She was no more attractive than Fern but she had a great deal more confidence and flirted uncontrollably when drunk. Erica was very popular, and Fern believed she always had been. She had long, thick red hair that sat beautifully around her face. Must have been her Celtic roots, Fern thought as she watched her friend promise a guy she would call him the very next day. Fern wasn't short on male attention either. But it wasn't why the girls had gone out that night. They just wanted to drink and dance and welcome in their second year of university in style. The two girls went home at 3am, when the music stopped and the students were kicked out. They got in separate taxis and went home.

Fern hated taxis. They always smelt of the person who had been in there previously and they scared her a little when she was on her own. But the driver was nice. He chatted away to Fern about how she reminded him of his own daughter and she smiled politely, as she listened.

Fern was relatively sober by the time she got in. She had resisted Erica's attempts at shots most of the night and had given up alcohol entirely by midnight so by the time she got home she was completely aware of her surroundings. She knew as soon as she walked up the staircase that something was wrong. The air felt tight and got worse with every step she took. It felt oppressive and unwelcoming.

By the time she reached the top of the staircase she was scared. Her instincts told her not to go further into the flat but what choice did she have? She looked into the living room and saw that nothing was unusual in there. She turned the light off that she had left on to deter burglars and plunged herself into complete darkness. She cursed herself for not thinking and opened her bedroom door. She was hit with a blast of cold air. Cursing herself again, this time for leaving a window open, she turned the light on. The cold air turned warm and Fern saw that all the windows were closed. The curtains were open though and she could have sworn that she had closed them before she left. She closed them and felt the cold air once more. She turned around and jumped. Her reflection in the wall of mirrors had startled her. She laughed at herself, turned the light off, took her clothes off and went to bed. She lay awake for what seemed like hours trying to work out where the cold air had come from.

Her imagination tended to take over in times like this and invent the worst case scenario. She had been on a school trip about seven years before she left for university and they had spent the night in a youth hostel. Fern had heard a noise while she was in bed and had convinced herself very quickly that it was a ghost. She didn't sleep all night and found out in the morning that the noise had been caused by a branch knocking on the window in the wind. She had felt very stupid that day.

She put the cold air down to the house being old and began to drift to sleep. She was somewhere between wakefulness and sleep when she heard a noise. It was like a faint tapping on glass. She turned toward the window and noticed, as she did so, that the sound was coming from the other side of the room. She sat up and turned towards the mirrors. As she did so she saw her reflection again. But this time it had changed. Her face was pale and her lips were black. Her eyes wide and staring. It was like the face she had seen in the well, but this time she was not scared. She stood up and moved closer to the mirror. With every step she saw her face changing. She watched as her smooth skin started to sink into her cheeks, making the bones in her face become prominent. The skin became grey and cracked making her look dead. She opened her mouth in horror and as watched herself transform, she saw her teeth were brown and rotten. It was the face from the well. She had been concentrating on the mouth of the reflection, and as she looked up she saw the dead eyes once more. They were clearer this time and this scared her. This time she could see the pupils, dilated and lifeless. She looked away and closed her eyes tight shut. She was close to tears but she forced herself to look back. She did, this time only seeing her face. She noticed the fear in her eyes and then mocked herself with a little laugh.

"Don't be so stupid!" She told herself. "It's just the alcohol."

Fern fell asleep that night at 4am perfectly aware that she was no longer drunk and that something was happening to her that she did not like. She decided just before she drifted off that she would talk to Erica in the morning, sure that she would rationalise everything for her.

Fern was less than happy with the response she received from her friend.

"My God Fern! You've got a bloody ghost!"

"What? Erica, that's rubbish!"

14

"Why? It makes sense, the cold air, the face you keep seeing."

"I've only seen it twice Erica."

"Yeah I know but you've only lived there for four days." Fern knew that Erica was right. She had seen the face twice in four days. and if the pattern continued she would see it tomorrow night as well.

"My friend from school moved to Aberdeen when we were ten. Her parents bought a bed and breakfast there and had a nice little business going. But, on her eleventh birthday, I went up, you know, as a surprise and something horrible happened. It was late, about 10 and we all heard a noise, her parents as well, coming from the basement. We went down thinking their cat may have got stuck and we saw that a door was open. A door that her parents had not been able to find the key for since they had moved. When we looked inside there were two skeletons inside."

"Oh my God! Who were they?"

"They had been servants about a hundred years ago and up until that day no one had known where they had gone. Turns out they had been murdered by the master of the house when he was unable to pay them anymore."

The story was made all the more frightening by Erica's Scottish accent. An accent Fern believed was made to tell horror stories with.

"Let me come and stay."

Fern was taken back.

"What? You want to stay at mine? After you just said it was haunted?"

"Exactly. It'll be fun!"

Fern agreed. It was hard for her to understand Erica's logic as the memory of the fear she had felt the night before was still fresh in her mind. But Erica had insisted that she stay over and Fern thought that it would be a good idea to have someone else in the flat with her. It would make it less scary if something happened again. After a short trip to Erica's to pick up some things, they went back to Fern's flat. Erica was excited and her mood made Fern a little more comfortable. Erica went in the kitchen and fetched a glass.

"If we leave this in the middle of the room overnight we can look at it in the morning. If it has condensation on it, we have a spectre."

Fern wasn't sure if that was true. Erica seemed to conclude her flat was haunted very quickly and she had never heard of this test before. But she was frightened. And she wanted something to help her understand what had happened the other night. Erica seemed to have experience with this sort of thing so Fern chose to go along with it.

The two of them spent the rest of the evening chatting about strange things that had happened in their lives. Erica seemed to win in the strangeness stakes. She had so many weird and wonderful stories to tell that Fern could not help but wonder if they were actually true. But it didn't really matter. Fern was enjoying listening to Erica's tales and it was a welcome distraction from worrying about what might happen later on.

Just before 11pm they went to bed. Fern offered Erica the bed and slept on the floor. Morning came and Fern could not see her friend. She walked into the living room and saw Erica.

"No condensation."

"What? Oh, the glass. That's a shame."

"No I expected that. It's tonight that will be the night."

Fern spent the rest of the day nervously wondering if Erica could be right. She didn't know whether or not she wanted something to happen later that day. If it did, it meant that she was renting a haunted flat, but at least she would know that someone else had seen what she had seen and she was not going mad. Fern had pondered whether it was the isolation that was making her have these dreams, or maybe there was something in the flat that was making her ill. The wallpaper was most likely riddled with mould.

The day rolled by slowly for Erica and rushed by for Fern. They did not find much to do that day. The tension was clear, and the flat had an atmosphere that made it hard for either of them to settle to an activity. Night fell and both girls felt nervous. Erica was still eager to see something but Fern could clearly see that it was nervous excitement. They decided that they would go to bed early as the activity only happened when Fern was in bed or asleep. This time Erica slept on the floor because she believed that the ghost was more likely to appear if things in the flat were as they had been. The two girls fell asleep surprisingly quickly. Erica slept peacefully but as Fern fell into a restless sleep, she began to dream once more.

This time she was in one of the classrooms. A nun was standing at the front teaching Latin to her class. The nun was tall and stood bolt upright. Her eyes were fierce and penetrating. Her voice barked Latin phrases without even a hint of kindness. Fern could not understand what she was saying and began to sink into her chair to avoid the nun's glances. A trick employed by all school children in times of crisis, Fern believed that it would save her here. She felt herself blush and saw that the nun was staring at her, shouting at her to stand. Fern did so and found herself muddling through some Latin phrases she knew from her English studies. She was saying Carpe Diem and trying to remember what it meant when she felt a sharp pain across her arm. The nun was standing next to her with a cane in her hand. Her voice was distant but Fern could tell that she was being told off for not listening. She watched at the nun bounced the cane up and down in her palm, waiting to unleash it on unruly girls.

Fern felt herself drift out of the classroom away from the nun and away from the cane. She was scared because she did not have control and did not know where she was going. As Fern floated down the corridor she saw a young boy outside, who could not have been more than thirteen, walking in the opposite direction. She knew him but did not know why. They did not exchange smiles as they passed but she saw something in his eyes. They reminded her of the eyes she had seen reflected in the well. The boy's face was very much alive but his eyes were dead. It was as if a light had gone out behind them. The boy was looking at her directly, but it was all automatic, there was nothing behind those blank eyes. As Fern turned her head away from the boy, she saw that she had come to the end of the corridor again and was going outside once more. She raced to the well, just like before, only this time she did not stop, as she got to the well she fell down into the water. She briefly saw the face of the girl as she hit the water. But this time she was not dead. This time she was crying. She had a look of unbearable pain across her face and suddenly Fern's head was filled with knowledge. The impact of the water had forced information about the girl into her mind.

Fern awoke once more with a start and whispered to herself.

"The girl is called Heather."

Fern looked over and noticed that Erica was not there. Fern was relieved as the dream had made her a little disorientated when she woke. She took a few minutes to gather her thoughts and left the room. Erica was in the living room looking disappointed.

"No condensation?" Fern asked, already knowing the answer.

"No condensation." Erica affirmed Fern's suspicions. "Any dreams?"

"No dreams." Fern lied to her friend without intending to, but when she thought about it afterwards she knew why. Fern had realised last night that the girl in her dream, Heather, was not a threat. In the last dream, Fern had understood something about her. This girl had suffered. She did not know what, but it made the fear go away a little. Plus, Fern was convinced that Heather was not willing to make herself known to another. She felt that maybe there was a reason that Erica had not experienced any kind of disturbance. Whatever Heather wanted, she only wanted Fern to be involved. Fern did not speak to Erica about Heather any more.

Fern was aware at this point that she was not alone in the flat. This understanding led to two possibilities. One, that Heather was a ghost trying to communicate with Fern, or that Fern was going insane. Fern chose to believe the slightly more acceptable fate that there was a ghost in her flat.

Since Erica's visit and the second dream, Fern hadn't experienced any more disturbances. She lived quite happily. Her excitement about living alone was only matched by her grades, which had improved noticeably since the first year. She found that because she had no one else to worry about, no bills to share or showers to queue for, she was a lot less stressed than her friends. Erica was no less intelligent than Fern, they had got similar grades in the first year, but Erica lived with four other girls and her grades were slipping.

"It's all Nat's fault." Erica exclaimed the day she got an essay back with a poor grade."

"What is?" Fern inquired.

"That my grades are falling. All I get, all day, every day, is the sound of dodgy dance music coming from her room."

Erica continued to talk but Fern's mind was elsewhere. Even after four weeks of peace in the flat, Fern had come to the conclusion that she had been experiencing some strange dreams because of the strain of living alone. She was enjoying the independent lifestyle but the adjustment had been quite hard at first. Maybe the disturbances had been stress related.   However, the mystery of Heather was intriguing Fern. She was not sure whether Heather was real or not but when she thought about it, she did have a lot of information about the girl already. She knew that Heather had gone to a Catholic school and had maybe lived where Fern was living now. Fern also theorised that Heather must have died tragically or she wouldn't be haunting the flat.

She thought about the time she had got hooked on watching 'real life' ghost hunters on TV. She had found it fascinating learning about the history of old houses. They never found hauntings in places where people died peacefully. There was always something tragic or painful or cruel that had taken place to keep the spirit tethered to this world. Fern thought about Heather and shuddered. She wanted to know her story but was unsure if it was a good idea finding out.

From her reflection, Fern determined that Heather was between eleven and thirteen years old, and so must have died at that age. Fern did not overlook the well. The other reflection of Heather, the one that had scared Fern so much, made it look as if Heather had drowned. With all this information, Fern was certain that she would be able to find out who this Heather girl was.

Fern began by going to the local history section of the university library. She found a few books that she thought may be useful and checked them out. Fern was pleased with herself. She had come to terms with the ghostly presence and was not running away from it. She thought she was handling everything very well. Of all the problems that she had imagined she would be forced to deal with by herself this year, a ghost had not been one of them. When she read through the books, there was a lot of useless information about local councils and monarchs visiting the city. In the last book she found what she had been looking for. She discovered that the name of the man who originally owned the house she was living in was Joseph McGinley. He lived there with his wife Margaret and their daughter Heather. Fern continued to read and found out that the couple had sold the house and moved all the way to London after their twelve year old daughter was killed in an accident at her school.

Fern sat back in astonishment. She was right. The ghost

of Heather McGinley was haunting her flat. Just then, Fern saw something out of the corner of her eye. She knew what it was, she had seen it before. She grabbed a nearby magazine, rolled it up and began hunting the spider she had seen run under her bed. Fern was a vegetarian and believed all animals had a right to live. Except if they had eight legs in which case she wanted them to die as painfully as possible. She had hated them ever since she was a little kid and her cousin had locked her in an outhouse, she had seen a couple of spiders as large as her hand only a few inches from her face. More than enough to develop a lifelong phobia. Fern moved the bed out of the corner of the room, saw the creature and hit it as hard as she could. She killed it and sat back on her bed, a little shaken but glad it was gone. Another victory for Fern's independent life. She decided she would call her dad and tell him she did it all by herself later that night when she noticed something right in the corner near to where she had killed the eight legged intruder. Part of the wall paper that had been used to decorate her room was pulled away and she could see paper underneath that had not been removed before it was redecorated. It had little pink flowers on it and she could just see something else. It looked like writing. Fern leant forward and pulled at the paper, not even stopping to imagine the reaction her landlord would have when he saw that Fern had destroyed the decorating. It came away easily and the writing was revealed. It said,

> Life brings us what we need,
> And takes away what we want.
> We live to love and love to live,
> But who of us can do,
> Everything we want to do
> And live the way we would love to.

It was a poem. Fern was amazed. She allowed herself to

wonder if it could have been written by Heather. It was possible, even though dozens of people must have lived in this flat between then and now. Fern knew as soon as she had seen the wallpaper that a child must have lived in the room and Heather was the only child of Margaret and Joseph McGinley.

Fern has drawn on her wallpaper once when she was a child and been told off by her mother. Clearly, this was not a modern behaviour. Looking at the handwriting closely it looked old, the script did not look like it was written by a modern hand. So it could have been Heather. But why had she written this poem on the wall of her bedroom?

Maybe Heather had been a writer. Fern hoped so because that would give them something in common. Fern had wanted to be a writer all her life and when she thought how young Heather must have been when she wrote this poem on the wall her respect and empathy for the young girl grew.

That night, Fern lay in bed and wondered about Heather. Most of all she wondered how she could find out more historical things about her. This puzzle was in Fern's mind as she went to sleep.

The third dream was the most interesting so far. Fern was not in the classroom or the corridor, or the wel. She did not know where she was. All she knew was that it was cold and she was scared. It reminded Fern of the outhouse full of spiders but this had no spiders in it. She felt around and worked out that she was in a coal shed. The black rocks around her smelt of it and, like the well it made sense for a school to have coal at this period in history. But all Fern's logic and understanding disappeared as the door swung open. Fern squinted at the sunlight that streamed in and hurt her eyes. The face she saw was the face of the nun who had been teaching her Latin. The expressionless face was asking her if she had learnt her lesson. Fern was adamant that she had, even though she did not know what lesson that was. She had got the impression from her last two visits here that you did not question the nuns. They were very much in charge and their superiority was not to be questioned.

The nun who was staring at Fern held herself tall and looked down her long thin nose. She leered at Fern with a level of disdain that she had never seen before. Her hands held the cane straight down by her side as if it were her loyal companion.

Just when she thought she couldn't take another second of looking at the nun, Fern blinked and was drifting through the giant doors once more and past the many classrooms. She looked in but this time the doors were closed and no one saw her as she drifted down the corridor. She went through a different door this time and found herself in the toilets. They were spotless, shining clean. Images of children scrubbing them until their hands bled swam into Fern's mind. Each toilet door was open and Fern saw that each one was as clean as the last. But there were some signs of dirt and decay seeping in at the corners. As she drifted into one of the cubicles she saw the mould creeping onto the green tiles on the walls. The smell of carbolic soap hit her as she entered and a wave of nausea came over her. She sat down with the seat down and felt herself crying. The weight of the pain was so great but Fern could not find the source of it. It was a pain that was deep and distant. It was like an ache in her heart and her stomach that welled up to her eyes, making her sob. She took out a small piece of paper from her bag and a pencil from her pocket and began to write the same words over and over again.

Trapped by the world, released by the word
Trapped by the world, released by the word

Fern was no longer confused about whether Heather had wanted to be a poet or not. It was clear that this was how she was able to express herself. It was the pain that had made her write the words. Fern wondered how such a young girl like Heather could possibly be aware of so much hurt.

Suddenly, without knowing how she got there, Fern was at the well. But she was not scared. She was happy. She looked into the water and saw a smile greet her. For the first time Fern could see how pretty Heather was. Fern felt herself smile back and the reflection smiled even more. Suddenly, Fern felt water on her face. She looked up and saw the boy from the corridor. He was splashing her with water from the well. She laughed and splashed back. Fern had never felt so happy, so joyful and free. This sensation did not last. As she turned away, to guard herself from the water, the scene changed. Her back was to the well and she saw the school girls and the nuns lined up again. Contortions of fear twisting their faces grotesquely. Fern quickly turned back and looked down into the well. The face she knew was Heather's but it was different. The pain from the toilet block came flooding back as she saw that face. The boy was still there. He was staring right at Fern with a look of horror. It was the same as he had been outside the corridor. He was alive but his eyes looked dead. The light had gone out. Fern was confused and she looked once more into the well. The water was gone. She could see a tunnel of nothingness. She did not know why but she felt herself drawn to the well. Before she could work out why, she was inside. At the bottom of the well with at least a dozen faces looking down at her. She was crying again, harder than before, the pain greater than ever, and she spoke. The voice was not distant this time and Fern heard herself clearly,

"You killed me!"

It was screamed up the well at the people looking down but they did not react.

Fern awoke and noticed that her face was wet. She had been crying in her sleep. She sat and thought about the dream. Had Heather been murdered? Now Fern was desperate to find out what had happened to Heather McGinley.

Fern moved her bed into the middle of the room. She wanted to keep the wall with the writing clear so she could contemplate the meaning of the poem. She was determined to figure out what Heather had meant. She had been a deeply disturbed girl that much was clear. But Fern wanted to know why. Fern cast her mind back. She could not think of a time when she was happier than when she was twelve. She had had lots of friends and spent every spare minute playing with them. Fern could not move the bed to the other side of the room because it would block the door so it had to stay in the middle. At this point however, Fern was not concerned with the aesthetics of her bedroom.

After rearranging her room, Fern phoned her landlord and asked if she could redecorate the room. She had realised after she had stripped the wall paper off the wall that she would get into trouble with the landlord if he found out. So she thought she had better get his permission the redecorate. He wouldn't know that she had already started. He said that was fine and if she kept the receipts from the paint she bought he would reimburse her for it when she had finished. With that sorted, Fern set to work. She did not want to redecorate but she did want to remove the wallpaper. She peeled more of the paper away from where Heather's writing had been and Fern was amazed at what was revealed. There was more. Fern discovered that the poem had been in the corner because the rest of that wall was covered in prose. This is what it said,

I am Heather. That is my name. I live in this house with my mother and my father. I want to die. No one knows who I am except Jacob. He understands because no one understands him. I will die soon because I have no choice. It is the only way I can be free. I will die before they make me stay inside.

Fern could not believe it. She thought that Heather had

been murdered but this made it look like she took her own life. But why would a twelve year old girl want to kill herself? A question that would haunt anyone. Fern sat staring at the wall for hours. She could not take it in. What did the last line mean? Who was making her stay inside and why was that so scary for her? As the sun went down, the light faded and Fern could no longer see the writing on the wall, she made herself go into the kitchen and eat something.

Fern decided to go to bed but her plans were brought to a halt when her door jammed as she opened it. She pushed with all her weight and managed to get inside. The bed had moved across the floor so the bed head was against the mirrors. Fern was frightened. Before, Heather had only done non-physical things. Now she had moved the bed across the room, and the bed was heavy as well. Fern moved the bed back across the room with some difficulty and put it back where it had originally been. Fern went to bed and fell asleep. She dreamt again of Heather but she was relieved when she saw that she was not in the school.

Fern did not recognise the house but she knew that she was in her flat before it was spilt into two homes. She realised she must have been in Heather's bedroom. There were pink flowers on the wallpaper and the original wall was still in place. There was a mirror on the wall and she looked into it. She saw Heather looking back. She was not smiling but she was alive. Heather said something to her but she could not hear. She spoke louder and it sounded to Fern as if she told her not to be afraid. She still could not hear the voice but the expression on Heather's face comforted Fern. She turned and walked out of the room. The room was a different way round to how it was in Fern's flat. The door out of Heather's room was where Fern's bed was placed. The room that Heather's door led to had been turned into a bathroom since the McGinley's had left. Fern saw that it had been a hallway that led to the stairs and the other rooms. She began to walk down the stairs and she noticed the pictures on the wall. They were of Heather's family, looking happy in family portraits. There was a large painting that was the centrepiece for the rest of the small collection. It showed Heather and her parents. They were dressed in their Sunday best and smiling. Fern looked closer and saw that the smile on Heather's lips was not matched by her eyes. When she reached the door that lead to the kitchen, Fern was suddenly inside. She was being taught how to make bread by her mother. Then she was shown how to wash before being given advice on marrying well.

Fern realised that Heather did not want a life in the kitchen. She did not want to be locked away in a dungeon like room with nothing to do all day other than labour for the wants of others. Heather was a free spirit; Fern understood this because she felt the frustration of the young girl as her mother took her through the arduous tasks of getting stains out of men's clothes and making sure that you bake the dough for just the right amount of time. Fern knew that Heather was a creative, intelligent person. She could feel it and she also knew that Heather wanted to be a writer. With this thought she was suddenly back at the school. She was standing in the field with all the nuns around her. They were all saying different things,

"That is no vocation for a young lady."

"Does that mean that you don't respect your mother?"

"You need to behave or you will go straight to Hell."

"God does not approve!"

All these things were going round Fern's head a mile a minute until she could take it no more and let out a deafening scream. When she stopped, she opened her eyes, she was in the well again. It was empty but this time there were no faces looking down. She heard a rumble above her head and she tilted her face up towards the sky. A droplet of water fell on her forehead and it began to rain. It got heavier and heavier, the well was filling up so quickly Fern did not even have time to panic. Soon the well was full and

Fern could not keep her head above the water.   She could feel herself drowning and closed her eyes. As she opened them she was out of the well once more. She looked down into the well but could see nothing. But she could sense that there was something down there, something that did not belong. She plunged her arm into the water and the grasp of cold fingers around her wrist. She pulled and Heather came lunging out of the water. Her mouth open and full of water, her face pale and lifeless, her eyes wide and empty. Fern had been too late. Heather was dead.

This last dream had really frightened Fern. She had forgotten about the bed moving across the room since she had awoken from her latest nightmare. Fern had not felt fear when she had seen Heather. All she had been able to feel was an indescribable sense of pain and regret. Last night, in her dream, she had witnessed the death of Heather McGinley. She had drowned in that well. Fern had to know more.

The normality of her existence seemed quite dull to her now. It was an effort to get herself out of bed and dressed for lectures. Fern pulled her jumper over her head and looked into the mirror. She mulled over the dream from last night. Heather had seemed so comforting a presence, so calm and gentle. But she had also experienced Heather's final moments and that was something she would never forget. The feeling of her mouth and lungs filling with water was horrific but to then have to stand and watch Heather go through that? Fern almost wished she could have stayed in the well and taken the suffering for Heather. She went to university and sat through her lectures without taking notes. The lessons they had to teach Fern at the university were paling into insignificance against the enormity of what she was experiencing at home. The only thing Fern thought about during her lectures that day was being finished and getting back to Heather. She went to the library again only this time she was looking for the school.

And she found it. It was called St. Agnes's School for Girls and was located just a couple of miles from Fern's home.

Fern hurried to her car and rummaged around in the boot to try and find the local road map her dad had put in there so she didn't get lost. She found it buried under everything else and opened it up. It took her a few minutes to find where she was and how to get to the school. It looked like a fairly straight forward drive so she got in her car and drove to find St. Agnes's. The drive lasted only thirty minutes but every second was agony for Fern. A million thoughts ran through her mind. What if the school wasn't there anymore? What if she turned up and all she saw was a patch of wasteland? Or worse, what if something had been built in the place of the school? Fern turned a corner and was forced to drive down a lengthy driveway at ten miles an hour.

Eventually she reached the end and saw a large, grey, overpowering building. Fern felt a moment of passing relief, it was still a school. Fern left her car and walked towards the school. The giant door loomed up before her. Fern was shaken, it was just like it was in her dream. She was forced to look up a long way before she saw the top of those intimidating doors. Fern walked cautiously towards them. There had been a smaller door added to the large ones to make it easier to gain access to the building. Other than that, it was exactly how Fern remembered it from Heather's dream. With each step that brought Heather closer to the school she felt a feeling of dread grow inside her. Fern's rational self told her that there couldn't possibly be anything to worry about. However, there was a part of Fern that believed she would open the doors and see nuns teaching Edwardian children when she went through the door. She stood staring at the door. There was a security buzzer next to it. She was just thinking of what to say to the person on the other side that would convince them to let her in when the door swung open. Thanks to good old-fashioned English manners they held the door for her and she stepped in. She turned left immediately and began walking hurriedly down the corridor. She looked in each classroom as she passed and saw teachers speaking to their pupils. They were not nuns any longer, she noticed with relief.

After passing eight classrooms she turned right. She had not even thought about where she was going when she had gone inside the school, but she knew as soon as she went out onto the playing field. She saw it. She began to run and eventually reached the well. It was fenced off but Fern was able to get over the gate that had been placed there to stop modern-day pupils from getting too close. 'Too little, too late' thought Fern as she took a deep breath and peered over the edge of the well, unsure what to expect. She saw nothing. The well was empty and Fern did not know whether to laugh or cry when she heard a voice behind her.

"May I help you miss?"

Fern turned round to see a rather stern lady looking at her. For a moment, she thought it was the nun from her dreams. But this woman, despite being stern had kindness around the edges and Fern relaxed.

"You do realise that you are trespassing on school grounds?"

"Oh. Sorry. I was researching the death of an old pupil here for my course at uni. I'm really sorry, I'll…"

As Fern was making her apologies and climbing back over the gate the lady interrupted her.

"You mean Heather McGinley?"

Fern was shocked but managed to nod her head.

"If you're interested in the facts miss, I can show you the school report from when she died.   We've had a lot of interest in her story over the years. Although it's hard for me to understand why. It all seems pretty straight forward to me."

Fern followed the lady back to the school and was taken into a room she had not seen before. Fern presumed it was the head mistress's office. There was a large oak desk in the centre of the room that made the entire office look grander than it was. The chair behind it was plastic with a cushion on the seat. Fern couldn't help but smile at the strange combination of furniture. She supposed it was quite characteristic of modern schools though. Not enough money to buy a chair to match a desk that had no doubt, from the look of it, been in that room since the school was built. She sat down and the lady, Mrs. Ward, the head mistress, handed her a photocopied sheet.

"I can't give you the original you understand."

Fern nodded as she began to read.

The death of Miss Heather McGinley.
Dated 12/10/1904.
The circumstances of this tragic death are not suspicious. The girl, aged twelve, decided to end her own life by descending down into the well and was killed by drowning. The girl's parents have been informed and will collect the body for burial as soon as it has been retrieved. The school has gone home to mourn and the undertaker has been informed of the sensitive circumstances.

It was signed and dated by a policeman; Fern could not read the name. She thanked the head teacher and left the school. She turned to look at the school once more before she got back in her car and went home.

The building was impressive, more Victorian workmanship. The corridor she had travelled down had large windows and she looked to where she had seen the boy in her dream. If there had been a path outside the school, it was no longer there. As she turned towards her car Fern thought about the well. Her look had been glancing but she had felt something which she didn't quite understand. It was almost like a pull, as if she needed to go back and have another look.

31

Fern didn't want to chance it with Mrs. Ward. She felt as if she had pushed her luck enough already today. Sitting in the car, Fern looked down at the announcement of Fern's death. It was so straightforward. No emotion to it. I suppose it had to be like that but Fern didn't want to think about Heather as a police report or a newspaper article. She wanted to know who she really was.

After returning home from the school, Fern decided it was time she found someone to help her with what had turned out to be a very complicated investigation. She knew that she had taken things as far as she could and now she needed someone who knew how to investigate these sorts of things. She now knew that Heather had killed herself but she did not really know why. There was something that was preying on her mind. Why had Heather shouted, "You killed me." to the faces at the top of the well? Fern decided to go her university. She was sure that there would be someone in the history department who would be able to help her.

Chapter Two

As Fern walked onto the university grounds she felt as though something had changed. It was almost as though she was walking just a little higher than everyone else. She was on autopilot. The people walking past her did not seem like individuals to Fern, they were just a mass of faces she did not want to engage with. Fern was focused entirely on Heather. The only thing she was able to concentrate on was finding more information on Heather McGinley. Fern was so consumed by her thoughts that Erica had to shout three times before Fern heard her.

"Fern. Hey Fern!" Erica eventually got through. "What are you up to?" I haven't seen you since our non-ghost experience."

Fern had to work hard to bring her consciousness back to the present to answer Erica coherently.

"I'm just going to the library. Research." The last thing Fern wanted was to get drawn into a conversation.

"Are you feeling okay? You look a little pale."

"I'm fine. Had a touch of the flu, that's all." Fern let out a small cough to authenticate this comment. Erica did not believe her. She was concerned for her friend. Fern looked withdrawn and despondent. Not anything like the Fern she knew. But Erica could not pin down what was bothering her friend.

"Okay, well I'll leave you to it. I'm going to the union again tonight. Monday is always good if you remember. Maybe I'll see you later."

"Yeah, maybe." Fern answered with no intention of going. She turned and left Erica with a look of concern on her face. Fern hadn't even realised it was Monday. She had missed two lectures that morning. Fern told herself it didn't matter. Heather was more important. She made her way to the library.

Fern went onto the university website and found three

history lecturers that specialised in local history. The first one she went to told her to forget the girl and get on with her studies. Just what she didn't need. Fern left his office in a bad mood. She thought that universities were supposed to encourage independent learning. She moved on to the next lecturer on her list but he wasn't in his office. The third one however was just what she had hoped for. His name was Professor James Morgan. He had worked at the university for twenty one years and had that dusty look about him that she thought older professors should have. He was quite plump and his thick rimmed glasses squashed onto his round face. His ginger hair sat on his head like it didn't belong there and he had a beard that he tangled up with a pen as he spoke. He could not believe how far Fern had got without consulting him earlier and to feed his intrigue she told him about the flat and the dreams.

He was the first person Fern had told everything to. It felt like a great release of emotion and her voice trembled slightly as she told him all about her traumatising dreams. Morgan was amazed. He could not believe his luck. As it turned out, he had researched Heather's death before when he was writing a book on St. Agnes's. The discovery he made about Heather McGinley had really made him think. He had never finished the book because of what he found out. He paused in his speech and he asked Fern a question.

"How far are you prepared to go for Heather?"

"As far as I need to."

Fern didn't even think about what consequences this answer may have had but she was more determined than ever to find out everything about Heather.

Fern followed Morgan down into the bowels of the library. Students weren't allowed down here unless they were doing postgraduate studies and Morgan explained, with a note of grief in his voice, that no one ever did a masters in local history at this university. They weaved their way through a maze of book shelves that were covered in

34

dust and stopped next to a large case of folders marked, 'McGinley.' Morgan passed them to Fern.

"Read these and come back to me when you've done."
Fern agreed and took them home. There was a lot to go through but she was happy to do it. She had to know the whole story. Heather had stopped Professor Morgan from writing a book about that school. This was too intriguing for Fern to be put off by the amount of research she would have to do to find the truth. She sat in the armchair and hardly moved from there for the next few days as she read what was in the folders.

Chapter Three

09/09/1903

Dear Lucy,

I am starting my first day of my new school today. This year should be fun because they are going to teach us Latin. I hope the nuns are nice. I have heard such horrid things about them but mother tells me they can't be as bad as all that. I have to leave now or I will be late but I will write about my day when I return.

Oh it was horrid! I was so looking forward to learning Latin and now it's ruined. My teacher, Sister Ruth made me stand up in front of the whole class and repeat what she had just said. I listened ever so hard but I couldn't remember the Latin words! It was dreadful and all the girls laughed. Sister Ruth said if I didn't listen again she would cane me. But I was listening Lucy, I was.

12/09/1903

Dear Lucy,

It is getting worse. Mother says that I must pay more attention in Sister Ruth's lessons. Mother was so cross with me that she punished me for the trouble I caused at school. Sister Ruth had already taken the cane to me earlier and just because I did not know the Latin words. She hit me across both arms and they are still sore now. I must stop writing because my arms are aching most terribly.

13/09/1903

Dear Lucy,

Well, things are looking up! I met a boy my age named Jacob today and it's all very secret. We girls are forbidden from seeing the boys at the school down the street from St. Agnes's because they aren't Catholic, but I didn't do it on purpose. I ran into him on the way home. Sister Ruth caned me again you see and I was desperate to get home and tell mother. Well, I ran right into Jacob and it turns out that he had been caned that day as well but he had got it for running in the corridor. He is ever so funny and I walked a fair way home with him. We said rude things about the sisters and his teachers . I have arranged to meet him tomorrow as well so we can swap stories about our horrid teachers. I know that I should not see him, and I fell terribly naughty meeting him in secret but we are very much alike and I feel like he makes Sister Ruth's cane less painful. He thinks Sister Ruth is mean just as much as I do and we have so much fun talking about our horrid schools.

17/09/1903

Dear Lucy,

Disaster! I did not get to see Jacob yesterday. Today I did not see him either because I was kept behind by Sister Ruth. She made me scrub the floors in the toilets. It was horrid in there and she gave me the smallest cloths to use.

I hate her. I wish she was dead! Sister Ruth is evil, Lucy. I know she is a nun and I should not say such things, but it is true! I don't pretend to understand the bible or what Christianity is but it can't be this. How can someone like her use the Holy teachings to be so cruel, so heartless? Mummy and Daddy used to tell me that the bible teaches us to forgive and be kind. Someone is lying to me, and I do not think it is my Mother and Father.

18/09/1903

Dear Lucy,

Mother spoke with me about my behaviour today. She said that she had been writing to Sister Ruth for the last week and had heard some very disturbing reports. I do not understand. I hate Sister Ruth! I have done nothing wrong. All I do to deserve this punishment is forget the Latin words. I cannot help it if I do not understand what I am being asked to do. I asked Mummy to try and see that I do listen and I do try very hard but she will only believe what Sister Ruth tells her. If I try and tell Sister Ruth that I don't understand she will cane me for being insolent. I am at an end with this. How can I be expected to learn if I fear the teacher?

19/09/1903

Dear Lucy,

Today was Bible studies. Sister Ruth insisted we all read a passage and make notes on its meaning and significance. The whole class were silent and Sister Ruth walked around us like she was a Queen. Head held high, moving the cane in her hands like she was preparing to strike at any moment. It was hard to concentrate on what she was saying with the ever present threat of that dreadful cane.

I read some of the passage and tried to do what she'd asked but I found it so dull. I started making little notes in the borders of the bible, ideas for stories and poems I could write later when I got home.

This was a big mistake! I assumed that Sister Ruth wasn't watching what we were writing but she was. When she saw me writing poems in the bible she broke the silence in the room with a deafening shout. I almost fell from my chair. She used my moment of shock to strike and I was pulled to the front of the class and caned I don't know how many times. The pain was unbearable and the whole class was watching. Normally, they use the cane outside in the hallway but Sister Ruth decided to punish me there, in front of everyone.

I cried for the rest of the day as I could not sit in my chair without a fresh pain making itself known to me.

12/09/1903

Dear Sister Ruth,

I am the mother of your pupil, Heather McGinley, and I understand that she is being quite unruly in class. I assure you that her behaviour is being punished at home as well as in school and we will put an end to this quickly.

Yours Sincerely,

Margaret McGinley.

13/09/1903

Dear Mrs. McGinley,

I am pleased that you have chosen to contact me before I was forced to write to you unexpectedly

It is true that I did cane your daughter to teach her the importance of listening to everything that I say in the lessons I give. I can tell that Heather is an intelligent girl and has quite a natural gift for writing eloquently. However, Heather does not pay enough attention in bible studies or Latin and so finds herself in a disadvantageous position. I hope that if you have further questions you will see fit to continue our correspondence.

Yours Sincerely,

Sister Ruth, Saint Agnes's School for Girls.

17/09/1903

Dear Sister Ruth,

I am sorry once again to trouble you with my daughter's problems but she has come home this afternoon with a frightful opinion of you and I think that it must be addressed. There is also another matter that I think is of the utmost importance and I believe that you are the correct person to inform. I took it upon myself to read Heather's diary. I discovered, to my horror that she has been associating with a young boy from the public school down the road. The boy is named Jacob but that is all I know. I do not wish for her to make any further contact with him and if you could aid me in this I would be very grateful.

Yours Sincerely,

Margaret McGinley.

18/01/1903

Dear Mrs. McGinley,

First of all, your daughter is as much a problem of mine as a problem of yours, so do not hesitate in involving me if you feel you need assistance. Also, you were right to read your daughter's diary as it has led to a probable disaster in her young life being averted. I will deal with the problem in communication with the public school and I will inform you of what is to be done.

In the meantime I would suggest that you speak with your daughter about her trouble at school and see if you can improve her attitude in general.

Yours Sincerely

Sister Ruth, Saint Agnes's School for Girls.

20/09/1903

Dear Lucy,

I do not know what to do anymore. I saw Jacob this morning before school and he told me that his Father had lashed him one hundred times the night before because the school had told him about all the trouble he had been in. When I heard this I did not think I was so badly off. My parents have never punished me in that way. But then I got to school. As I walked up to the front door of the school they opened before me and I was given such a start when I saw that Sister Ruth was standing in the doorway looking right at me. I stopped as I was just in front of her and she said the strangest thing to me, she said,

"There is only one thing to be done with girls like you."

I was very confused as I did not know what I had done so wrong as I had not even got inside the school building yet. I glanced up at the clock tower and saw that I was not late so I asked Sister Ruth what I had done that was wrong. She bent down so her horrid old face was as close to mine as she could get it and whispered in my ear,

"You know."

But I didn't, and just as I was about to say that Sister Ruth took a hold of my ear and dragged me into the school courtyard. I did not know why I was going here but I did see that all the girl's from my class were outside and watching what was going on. The courtyard was a place I had never been and I did not understand why I was being taken there because the only thing in the courtyard was the coal hut and an old plough that had been there unused for what must have been years because it had gone rotten from the rain. The walls around the courtyard were high and no sunlight would touch the floor.

The classroom where I am taught is next to the yard and I had spent moments looking out at the two lonely items, sitting together in the wide empty yard. Sister Ruth stopped and allowed me to drop to the floor. My hand shot to my ear instinctively. It was throbbing after Sister Ruth had dragged me all the way to the courtyard. I sat on the floor trying to decide what hurt more, my ear or my legs. They were grazed from when I had landed on the hard floor. I wanted to find a way to soothe my wounds but I knew that with Sister Ruth in control of my fate, that would not be allowed to happen.

She opened the lid of the coal shed and told me to get in. My first reaction was to say no but this enraged her further. She picked me up with one arm and dropped me over the lip of the shed. I tumbled in, hitting the cold, dirty floor with a dull thud. Casting one final glance of disgust at me, she slammed the lid.

In the utter darkness I heard the scratching of something being placed on the top of the shed and then silence fell about me. I was terrified. I felt around me to see how much room I had and felt the hard lumps of coal all around me. I put my hands up to the lid and pushed. It would not move so I pushed it harder. Still nothing! I sat down defeated and began to cry. I did not stop crying until I ran out of tears. Then a terrible thirst took me and I tried to shout for help. But my throat was so dry that I could not make a sound. I started to cough with the effort and it would not stop for some time. I thought I might be sick but it calmed and my mind turned back to my injuries. I was in terrible pain and I thought I might die before I was released. If I was to be released at all. My ear was aching and throbbing. My legs were sore and although the cuts were only small I feared that the dust of the coal would irritate my wounds. Maybe this was how they got rid of naughty little school girls. I began to cry dry tears again and all I wanted was to go home and sleep in my bed.

I could not tell how long I was in the coal shed, but when I was let out it was dark. I needed water so badly but Sister Ruth just opened the lid and told me to go home. As the lid was opened I saw the expression on Sister Ruth's face and I saw a faint smile. As my eyes adjusted her face returned to its usual grimace. Maybe she had not smiled after all. When I returned home I discovered that my mother was not angry at Sister Ruth. In fact I think she was pleased! She thought it was a punishment well deserved.

I went to my room with a mug full of water and sat staring at the wall. I hated the wall paper and had wanted to tear it down for years but Mother had not allowed me to. I reached down and took out a book of blank pages. A little like you were at first, Lucy! I decided that I was to write poems and short stories in it so that when I was grown up I could sell them and live independently without having to worry about learning Latin or behaving like a good girl should. I could run away to another town and be the rebellious girl who lives on her own. What would people say? I would write stories and sell them to anyone who wanted them. I think it is a good idea.

22/09/1903

Dear Lucy,

As if my punishment at the hands of Sister Ruth wasn't bad enough my Mother and Father decided to do something even worse to me!

They have taken all but my school books and pencil away. My little book of pages that I had barely started writing in has been taken away. And they are checking that I am not writing poems or stories in my school books. I am glad I hid you, Lucy or I would have lost you too. Mother found you once so I am being extra careful where I keep you now. I am writing this in the dying light of the day so I don't draw attention with a candle.

Of all the punishments so far I think this is the worst, I can recover from canings and from being locked in a hut with no light. I can live with a teacher who hates me but not being able to write down how I am feeling is unliveable.

I must ensure you are never found, Lucy. You may be the only friend I have left after all this is over and I cannot afford to lose you.

I may start writing on the walls if I end up with no other option.

02/10/1903

Dear Lucy,

Mother and Father sat with me today and explained how disappointed they are in me. Father was kinder than Mother. He said he understood that I loved to write and it was ok to but that it was getting in the way of my studies. This, he could not allow to happen. I needed a good, well rounded education to please my future husband.

I thought this was a strange comment, why would I need an education to be a wife. But Father insisted it was necessary. I needed to maintain good standing in the church and be able to support my husband in his endeavours.

I sat and listened to everything they said and tried to smile and seem like I agreed. I need them to stop checking my books so I can write more again. I know I can use your pages, Lucy but what happens when you run out? What happens when there is no more space to write?

The talk with Mother and Father has left me feeling more frustrated than ever, I wish I could make them understand. I feel as if they have planned my life out for me with no thought to what I might want myself. I can't abide the thought of living my life for someone else. They talk of a husband like that will be my job, my livelihood. Surely, that is not all the expect me to live for. Surely, that is not all they can see in my future. I feel as if there is so much more for me to offer, on my own, as a woman.

There must be a way of making myself understood.

The following are three of the poems that were handwritten by Heather in the book she noted in her diary on 20/09/1903. Professor James Morgan had highlighted them as the most important poems in the book. Heather had only had this book for two days but she had written dozens of poems and a couple of very short stories in it.

Why?
Blacker than night,
Colder than ice.
I sit and ask God, why?
Her holy spite
Punished my childhood vice
I sit and ask God, why?

My hands are cut
And my knees bleed
I sit and ask God, why?
This hellish hut
This evil deed.
I sit and ask God, why?

My throat went dry,
My life was waning.
I sit and ask God, why?
I close my eyes
Life is draining.
I sit and ask God. WHY?

Three things I believe.
At first that heaven will reward.
Forgive my deeds that are untoward.
Second, Hell will punish her evil.
She is wrong not to fear the devil.
Third and last I will live long and well.
Once I escape this holy Hell.

Sister Ruth.
Sister Ruth it is quite true,
Would rather like to punish you.

She laughs as you feel unholy pain,
And shouts for it again and again.

Sister Ruth it has been said,
Would fair much better if she were dead.

I will dance upon her ugly grave,
And ensure her soul, God does not save.

Fern thought this last poem was very childish but could
see why Morgan had highlighted it. Fern had only read a
fortnight's worth of Heather's life but she was already
beginning to understand how much turmoil she had been
in. Heather had described the coal hut very well but it was
not necessary for Fern. Heather had taken her there in one
of the dreams and she had felt exactly what Heather had
described. Fern took a minute to gather herself together; she

sat back in the arm chair and stretched her feet out. In doing this, she knocked a pile of the papers on the floor. She cursed and bent over to pick them up. She stopped with her hand over the papers. The diary was open on a page marked 02/04/1904. That was a long time after what she had just read but Fern could not resist reading it. It was written in the same handwriting but this page was messier. Fern had been impressed with the clear lettering that Heather had in the first few entries but this was clearly written in a hurry. Or at least with no care for neatness.

02/04/1904.

I am at an end. What is this world? I have spent the last few months trying as hard as I can to do well for Sister Ruth and my parents. I even managed to only get the cane twice a week since March. But I suppose it is my fault. I have written in here about my growing friendship with Jacob. He is my only friend as none of the girls from my school want to associate with me. He has not been in much trouble either recently, mainly because we have got very good at hiding our meetings. I lie to mother and tell her that I have a friend from school called Jane and I tell her every Saturday that I am going to play down at the river with her. Mother believes me of course and I go for hours at a time to play with Jacob. Those hours together are very important to me. Jacob is my only friend and he is the only person who I can show my true self to. When I laugh, he laughs with me. When I cry, he cries with me. When I am angry, he calms me down and when I am upset, he cheers me up. I believe that we will always be together. We have to hide our friendship, but I am prepared to hide it if it means we can be together.

Last Saturday we ran around the field behind the school and when we grew tired we threw rocks and pieces of mud from the farmer's field down the well. It was fun because the well didn't have very much water in it and we threw them down and then waited for the distant splash when they hit the bottom. Then we laughed at all the dirty water the nuns would have to drink.

When we got tired of the well we laid on the grass beside it and laughed about how ugly the nuns and the teachers are. We wondered if that is why they became nuns and teachers in the first place, and if it was a necessity to be ugly to become one. We talked like that for hours. Clouds began to sail over our heads and we argued over what animals they looked like. I said the biggest one looked like a rabbit but stupid Jacob said it was a horse. It was a rabbit.

When we got hungry we went home and I told Mother that I had had a lovely day with Jane. She made a comment about how nice it was that I was making friends and spending time with respectable girls rather than troublesome boys and I went upstairs. She was so desperate for me to reform and fall in line that she was far to eager to tell me how much better it was for me to be with Jane instead of Jacob. I agreed with her and, allowing a small smile onto my face, I walked away.

I wrote a short story in my school book about a young girl and a young boy being chased by ugly people who wanted to kill them and then I was called to dinner. I tore out the pages with the story in them and hid them under my bed for safekeeping.

Mother had prepared a feast that day and I ate a lot because I had been running all day with Jacob. My Mother and Father had a jovial conversation about something, but I do not know what. They seemed to have moved on from punishing me for writing. I was much better at hiding it and the trouble from school was less and less frequent. It was tiring keeping up with everything and still pursuing my dream of writing but I am stubborn enough to keep going.

I know that my perseverance will pay off. When I think about the bad experiences of my life now I try to think about turning them into a story in the future and having hundreds of people read them. How satisfying it is to think of people learning the truth of my life.

On Sunday I went to church and I saw Sister Ruth. I guided my parents towards a pew that was as far away from her as I could get. I saw enough of her at school, I did not need to see her at church as well. I was glad to not be able to see Sister Ruth's face but I could tell that she was sneering. She was always sneering. I wondered to myself what it would take to make her smile. If being in the house of God did not make a nun smile, then goodness only knows what would?

The service was boring as usual and I was not interested in hearing what the priest had to say to me at the end when he shook hands with my Mother and Father. I took little notice when Sister Ruth approached us. I hoped that she would just continue to walk past us but she didn't. She stopped to talk to Mother. I pretended not to but I listened to every word that was said. I was surprised when Sister Ruth said I was improving daily. She said I was requiring less correction and if things continued I would be a respectable girl by the time I left school. Despite the lack of warmth in her voice it was nice to hear it, and I allowed myself a little smile at the compliment.

It appeared to me on the Monday morning, however, that it had been a rather false sentiment. As soon as Sister Ruth walked into the class room she ordered everyone to sit except me and I had to recite a poem in Latin that we had read the previous week. I could not get past the first line. I had really tried, you must believe me, to learn the stupid language but I just couldn't get it right. I tried to tell Sister Ruth this as she marched over to me and by the time she was next to me I was crying for her to take mercy. She didn't and she dragged me from the classroom out into the hall and as I watched her arm, cane in hand rise above her head, I closed my eyes and braced myself for the pain. It was worse than the previous times, and it was because she was not caning me but she was beating me. The cane fell again and again and I fell to the ground in agony. I held my arm with my left hand but she just caned my hand so I had to let go. Pain was screaming through my body, and I had to do my best to stop from crying out. I turned over so that my arms were under me and she began to hit me across my back. It is Wednesday now, two days after the beating, and I still cannot lie on my back, it hurts so much.

On Tuesday I did not go to school because I was crying from the pain so much that my Mother called for Doctor Finlay. He told my mother to bathe my wounds and return to school the following day. Neither my Mother or the Doctor were sympathetic, they talked at length about how I needed to learn my lesson if I didn't want to be caned. I needed to be better behaved and take more care of my studies. Doctor Finlay's wife was a devotee of Latin and read poems frequently in the language.

After that I was forced to endure a whole day of my Mother telling me that it was my own fault, and if I would just listen then I would have been fine. How infuriated she was with me for not just doing as I was asked. She even brought me extra Latin texts to try and help me to learn. I had run out of energy to argue this point and went to bed without supper.

When I went back to school this morning, I was aware that I would be punished for missing school the day before, even though I had a letter from Doctor Finlay explaining why it would have been impossible for me to have attended. Sister Ruth was not convinced.

"If you are unable to sit for the class you simply stand. This is unacceptable and you will be punished accordingly."

One of the girls, I do not know her name, made a comment that it was unfair. Sister Ruth heard her and she was promptly caned. That was the last time any one of the girls made a comment on my behalf. I could see in their eyes that they wanted to help me. This was of no use to me of course, but I could see in their faces that they were scared and had no idea how to help. The classroom was a prison of fear.

I was taken out into the field behind the school and marched towards the well. I was more scared of this punishment, whatever it was, than any of the previous ones, because I did not want this well to hold any bad memories for me. It was where I played with Jacob and that was all I ever wanted it to be. It would be truly evil of Sister Ruth if she were to ruin this place of joy for me. But any thought in my mind that she would take this into account, even if she had known how special this place was to me, was soon dismissed as I recalled the nun's previous punishments.

Sister Ruth took me to the edge of the well and said that while she was teaching the other girls Latin I was to count how many bricks there were on the inside of the well. From the bottom, all the way up. She left with no further instruction and I was left a little confused. How could I count the bricks at the bottom of the well if could not see them. The sun was never able to illuminate the very bottom and I knew that it was deep because I had thrown all those stones down there with Jacob. Probably not as deep as it used to be with all those stones down there I thought with a little laugh.

I decided that the only way to do what Sister Ruth had asked was to climb down into the well and count as far up as I could, then mark where I had got up to somehow, climb back out and then count from the top. Simple, I thought. It was not simple. I climbed down the well quite successfully, and it had not been as deep as I had thought, and the chain that held the bucket was sturdy and secure. At the bottom I set my feet down and I could stand with the water just up to my thighs. It was freezing cold and I regretted this tactic as soon as I felt the water hit my legs. I could see all the way up to the top so I decided to count from the water line up. There were two hundred and thirteen bricks. I made sure by counting them twice and got the same number again. Feeling pleased with myself I started to climb out. I got just about half way up when I slipped. My legs had gone numb from the cold water and my whole body was shivering. Climbing up was harder in the first place but with the added element of the cold it was impossible. I was hanging on with one hand and could feel the cold steel slipping quickly out of my grasp. I fell and landed badly, water shooting up my nose and then into my mouth as I tried to catch my breath. I tried to stand up, but I couldn't find the bottom. I flung my arms around and hit the sides of the well several times before managing to right myself and stand. I was wet now from head to foot and the cold was creeping deep into every part of my body.

I heard a shout from the field and realised that the

Latin lesson must have finished because all the girls and Sisters were coming out on to the field for a break. I looked up and saw that Sister Ruth was looking down the well at me with her familiar sneer and before too long, so were all the girls who had just been in the Latin lesson. All I heard was a 'tut' sound from Sister Ruth and an occasional laugh from one of the girls. Sister Ruth shouted down to me.

"If you are silly enough to get yourself trapped down there then you can stay there and think about what a stupid girl you are until the end of the next lesson."

I shouted up to tell her that I was cold, my teeth chattering and whole body shaking as I did so but she had walked away before she heard me. The girls took a last look and then turned away to play. I was left alone.

A million thoughts ran through my mind while I was in that well. I was unable to think clearly and my mind began to turn to dark thoughts about Sister Ruth. How could I hurt her in the same way she had hurt me? How could I make her feel fear and pain like she had caused me? How could I end her life?

I thought the best day to do it was on a Sunday after church. Jacob and I could hit her over the head with a bible until her eyes popped out of their sockets and her brains went all over the floor and she was dead, dead, dead, and then we could run away together until we found some nice grown-ups to look after us. Grown-ups that cared about children and listened to what they wanted. Or, I could take her cane from her and stick it down her throat until she spits her blood up and chokes to death on the classroom floor. All the other girls would be so stunned that I could easily run away without any of them stopping me. I imagine one or two of them at least would step out of my way to let me pass. The best way by far was the latter idea. If I was patient, the way Sister Ruth had taught me to be, then I could wait until the autumn and then the well will be full to the top. I will run into her classroom in the morning and tell her that a girl had fallen in the well, then, when she is desperately trying to see the girl, I push her in. There is no way a fat old trout like her would be able to keep her head above water. Especially if I was holding her under. These thoughts were proving very pleasant as I paced around the well in a desperate attempt to warm up when I was hit on the head by a length of rope. A yell told me to tie it firmly round my waist. I did so although it was desperately hard to tie a knot with hands that had gone numb some time ago, and was rescued by the groundskeeper of the school.

I was taken into the kitchen and told to sit by the fire to dry out. It was a blessing as I was left alone in there. The pain of sensation returning to my hands was worse than the cold making them numb. I knew it would get better but it was agony.

All I thought about that afternoon was the well and the water and my hand pushing down on Sister Ruth's head so she could not come up for air. I thought about Sister Ruth as she taught the girls in the class room and I pitied them. Did they have any idea that she was evil? Or did they just think it was normal? They sat and listened to her and took in every word that she said. The poor misguided girls. I wondered when they would realise the truth about the nun. If they ever did. I went home and I have not stopped writing since, I have got angrier and angrier with every word. Whose justice is she carrying out? Because I am sure that it cannot be God's.

Fern sat back in her chair. She could not believe what she was reading and she did not know how to react. Questions raced through her mind. But no answers would come to her for a long time. Had Heather killed herself or been murdered? Had she killed Sister Ruth before she died? What did this have to do with her and what did she have to do with this information? Fern had realised by this point that she had things in common with Heather. Some of the things Heather had said, reactions she had made, opinions she had formed. All of which Fern felt she would have made and felt if she had been in Heather's position. Is that why Heather had led her to this information? Because she felt she would understand. Fern decided that the only way to find out was to carry on reading. But she was scared. She did not want to read anything more but she knew that she must. It was the only way she was going to find the answers to her questions.

She decided to take a break and get a drink. Fern stood in the kitchen waiting for the kettle to boil thinking about what it must have felt like to be stuck down that well. A girl, freezing cold and lonely. No idea when, how or if she would get out. Tears pricked the corners of her eyes. She jumped as the kettle clicked off and she made herself a cup of tea. Walking back into the living room Fern felt a sudden coldness creep into her entire body. It was so intense it felt like she was cold down to her bones. She felt so cold she shivered and drew the cup of tea closer to her.

The feeling of cold was so intense she felt the need to grab her blanket and sit down with her tea to try and warm up. Nothing seemed to penetrate the cold. She sipped her tea hoping this would warm her but no sooner had the warm tea left her mouth, it had turned cool and made her shiver even more.

The feeling passed and Fern felt the need to carry on reading.

She picked up the diary and began to read from where she had left it.

07/04/1904

I now know, after the events of last week that I must leave this place. I am not safe. I am thinking much more clearly now, and I have realised that it is not just Sister Ruth. It is everybody who is trying to hurt me. Allow me to explain.

After the incident with the well, my Mother and Father were summoned to the school and we were all asked to sit down with Sister Ruth and the Mother Superior of the school, Sister Mary. During this meeting I heard a lot of Sister Ruth's embellishments about my behaviour and I watched as my Father's face grew redder and redder with anger, and my Mother turned a similar colour with embarrassment. Eventually, the adults in the room had the good sense to ask me about the situation.

I tried in vain to explain that I could not do the work in Sister Ruth's Latin class because it was too hard. But the task of defending myself was made increasingly difficult by the tuts of disagreement I got from Sister Ruth. At the end of this part of the conversation I was asked a question by Sister Mary, a woman who I actually did like, despite her being on the side of Sister Ruth. Maybe it was the idea that she was superior to Sister Ruth that made me like her slightly more. She asked me a question that I was not expecting.

"What is it that you expect to do with your life when you leave us here at Sister Agnes's?"

I was a little shocked at this question. It was rare, in fact it never happened, that a Sister here would think of asking what you wanted to do, instead they usually just told you. I gathered my thoughts quickly as I saw this opportunity as a way of finally making them understand me. I stood up and said as clearly as I could. With as much conviction as any person could manage I said,

"I want to be a writer."

This was greeted with a silence that I did not like. I sat back down, avoiding making eye contact with any of those in the room. I could feel heat coming from my Father who was sitting at the side of me. The silence continued as I kept my eyes fixed on my knees.

When you made a statement like that and no one says anything, you don't tend to feel very comforted. I had done what was asked and laid down my heart. Why did they not say anything? Eventually, they all started talking. To each other though, not to me, I was left in between the four of them feeling as if they could not even see me. I was left wishing that they couldn't. At least that way I could just have walked out then, and I would not have had to listen to what was said next.

I stood and listened in disbelief as these four people who claimed to know and care about me discussed how they were going to stop these silly ideas about writing getting in the way of what I was supposed to do in my life. My Mother was outraged that I did not want to follow her into a life of servitude and become a housewife. The two nuns were ashamed that they had failed to instil the correct sensibilities of a young woman into me and my Father was greatly angry that his only daughter was not willing to dedicate her life to pleasing a man, and making him a grandfather.

I discovered during this meeting, which by this point I had no part in, that my parents had already found an eligible man for me to marry when I was sixteen. Sixteen! That is only four years in the future. How can I get married then? I have so much to do.

First of all I have to write all about Sister Ruth so that maybe I can warn people, or at least help them to understand that she was an evil woman disguised as a holy one. This, in my opinion, is the worst evil of all.

They discussed me for what seemed like an eternity. I was sitting but I felt as if every part of my body was tense even though I was still. I felt as if even the smallest movement on my part would draw their attention to me, and all the shame and disappointment that was flowing between the four other people in the room would be fired directly at me. I could not face that. It was bad enough that I had to listen to it. The talk did not cease. The subject did not change. It was agony to hear it. I tried not to listen. I tried to think of different things. Happy things.

My mind flitted from Jacob to poetry, to leaving these walls, and these people who by trying to do the best thing for me were actually doing the worst thing possible. I even found myself thinking that it would be better for me to be back down the well than in here. At least as I was alone in there. The fewer people around you, the less there are to hurt you.

I was snapped back to unpleasant reality when my mother began to sob. Sister Ruth had apparently suggested the rather unpopular option that I be sent to a correctional facility for unconditioned girls. My father had risen to his feet and was informing Sister Ruth with great insistence that she was to send me to no such place. I did not know whether to be relieved or not. Maybe a change of evil would be better than suffering the same evil over and over again. I even dared to imagine what it might be like. I expect I would have a lot of chores, this I didn't mind as it was thoughtless work which would give me plenty of time to think of stories. But then I also imagined there would be no paper and pencils for me to use in my spare time, if there was ever any spare time at all.

Sister Ruth, very much out of character, apologised to my father and he sat down. A few minutes later my parents stood and escorted me from the classroom. There were idle farewells and I departed. When I arrived home my mother stopped me from entering my room and insisted on conversing with me for some time about how satisfying it was to be a good housewife. How fulfilling it was to support a good husband in a good job and bear and raise his children. I suffered her for around an hour, after which I was allowed to go to bed. I have been writing now for some time. I have written as quietly as possible. Now my parents know that I have ambitions beyond the station they have assigned to me I must do my best to hide this diary. If they find it, I fear they will destroy it.

Fern suddenly realised what Heather had meant when she said she would die before they made her stay inside. That writing on the wall had confused her but now she understood. Heather had wanted to be a writer but her parents and the school were trying to make her become a housewife. Fern was appalled, she didn't care how long ago this was, dictating what a person should do with their lives is wrong. How could two people bring a child into the world and then not want her to fulfil her dreams? It was beyond Fern's comprehension. She could plainly see how intelligent Heather was. How come her own family could not?

She thought about her Father and how he had insisted on buying her a car for university. "I don't want you driving around a new city in some old banger." He had seen her looking at cars for sale and she had circled all the cheapest ones. He had taken the newspaper off her and circled some more expensive, but still reasonable ones and told her to pick which she wanted to go and look at. There was no ulterior motive with her dad, he just wanted her to be safe. Fern sat and thought how lucky she was to have been born into an age of relative tolerance and read on.

The entries in the diary were becoming sporadic and the next one was dated in August. Fern read on.

18/08/1904

Dear Lucy,

I am happier now, more so than I can ever remember being. I am on a break from school over the summer months and I have welcomed it. When I return to school in September I will no longer be taught by Sister Ruth because she teaches the class of children that are a year younger than me. I will have a new teacher and I am excited that I may be able to begin to enjoy my school work instead of loathe it.

My parents are insistent that I marry Joseph Walsh when I am sixteen. They hosted a supper for him and his parents to come along and see me. I was dressed up like a doll and told to be quiet and smile at them. Mother made a point of not talking about writing or getting into trouble at school. The Walsh's didn't want an ill-behaved and foul tempered woman for their son.

Matthew Walsh works with my father at the bank but he is more important than father. Joseph will follow in his father's footsteps and become more important that most of the men there. It struck me that Joseph is trapped too. He has a path laid out before him as have I. I wondered if he was as miserable as I was.

My parents have arranged for us to be married as there are very few Catholic families in the area and the Walsh's are a nice family who we see at church every Sunday. It was the perfect match for the families concerned and I would be very comfortable and would probably be able to afford a maid to help with the housework.

The Walsh family are wealthier than we are. I have been told many times that he will make my life better and allow me to live the life of a perfect wife at home with as many children as possible. This has always been an issue with my parents. They only have me which is unusual in the families we know from church, most have many more. Joseph is the eldest of 11 and I think mother and father think that means I will bear that many as well.

I cannot bear the thought of it. Shackled to the duty of motherhood for years on top of years. No time to pursue my passion of writing. I can already feel the weight of responsibility and I am still only 12 years of age. This can't be all there is for me. Can it?. Child after child. Having eleven children must require being with child most of the time. It sounded exhausting.

I have been seeing Jacob a lot in the time off that we have had in these warm months, and I have treasured the time. We still meet in private which becomes harder and harder as our parents have been keeping a close eye on what we have been doing. We do not visit the well anymore but Jacob understands why. His uncle was the groundskeeper who rescued me and he told the family all about it. But I will not dwell on that unhappy time. I am looking forward now to a more happy time and I am confident that I will fulfil my dreams and write when I am older. Even if a do have to get married, I will find a way. I am sure that I am not the first person to have faced such obstacles as these. I have been musing over my situation and now believe that I am destined to write.

I will make it so. It is hard now to see because I am so young, but now that school is looking more hopeful I will just have to weather the storm and write all about it as a woman.

Fern could not help but smile as she read this. The little girl was a child again. All those dark thoughts had disturbed Fern. Sometimes as she was reading Heather's diary, she forgot that it was being written by a twelve year old girl. All that despair and frustration. It was not easy to imagine how a girl so young could feel those emotions the way Heather had described. When she read this however, she was pleased. Heather was happier and looking forward to a long and happy life. With this thought in her head Fern relaxed. She slumped down in her chair and felt her heavy eye lids slide shut. She had not slept for twenty hours and this moment of relief allowed her to drift off happily.

The dead face. Again. It rose up through the water and looked straight at Heather. Two hands, pale and rotten with death, rose out and grabbed Fern's face. With an incredible strength, they pulled Fern down into the water and she was drowning. As Fern gasped and desperately tried to swim back to the top, the hands pulled her towards the face. Fern's head was inches from Heather's. "Don't forget."

She woke up. The room was chaotic. All the papers were flying around the room and Fern wondered if she was still dreaming. The pages of the diary were being turned over furiously and all the notebooks, letters and reports were circulating around the room as if there was a tornado in Fern's living room. Fern rubbed her eyes desperately trying to see what was causing the chaos. She could feel the cold wind again. The one she had felt when she had seen Heather's face in the mirror one night. Fern suddenly grew scared as she recalled that night. She sat bolt up right and the papers fell to the floor. The diary lay still and was in front of her on the table. It was dated, 10/10/1904. Two days before the death of Heather McGinley.

10/10/1904

How could this have happened? Sister Ruth is killing me. She is killing me! Why did she ask Sister Mary to keep me in her class an extra year? I do not need to be kept back with the children. I did well enough. Better than some of the girls in my class and they all went on to the next year. I hate Sister Ruth, I hate her! She hates me also, that is why I cannot understand what she has done. Surely she was as eager to see me leave her class as I was to leave it!

I had to stop writing. But I am calmer now and I feel like I can write more legibly. I have now decided that I must keep this diary as well as I am able. It has long been my dream to be a writer and I now know that this diary may be the last thing that I write. I do hope that it will be read some time by a man with the means to have it published. I was kept back a year because Sister Ruth asked that I be. I did not agree but Sister Mary did; I do not believe that my opinion matters much to these people. Sister Ruth said that I must remain in her class this year so I must stay. Even when I expressed my fear of her cruelty and explained some of Sister Ruth's more ghastly punishments, Sister Mary did not take heed. She merely waved my complaints away as if they were a nuisance to her.

It is hard for me now, in this moment of odd calmness that has taken me now to express the terror that has fallen upon me. I fear for my soul as I try to be good and true to the Lord God, but I do not see that that would do any good. Sister Ruth prays for four hours a day and she will surely go to Hell. But she is certain God has a place for her in Heaven. I would not want to go anywhere she is after I am dead. If I could be sure she will go to Heaven, I would be the most evil girl in England for that would ensure that I would never see her again. Hell would be an eternal bliss for my soul as long as I do not see Sister Ruth there.

The day of classes I endured did not go too badly, except for the unavoidable caning I received for my mistakes in Latin. I do not wish to speak or read or even write in Latin in my life, so I simply do not understand Sister Ruth's insistence that I learn it so thoroughly.

I saw Jacob after school and we strolled along the streets to his home together. I was happier then because he was so pleased to have advanced in his schooling. He was allowed to move on and he now has a more pleasant teacher. I listened to him talk about this teacher for so long that we had concluded our walk before I had a chance to tell him about Sister Ruth. I am glad though. He was so happy and I did not want to burden him with the news of Sister Ruth.

It was so hard to walk alongside him and not burst out with my grievances, but I did not say a word about Sister Ruth. It was very difficult for Jacob last year and I do not believe that he would wish to listen to my worries when his mood was so good. I allowed him to assume I was also in a better position than last year. I think it best that I did not tell him. I do not believe that I will tell him ever. I will sit out this year and be as good as I can be. I will take any punishment with as much dignity as God can give me. For perhaps this is nothing more than a cruel test. Maybe God saw me and thought I needed to prove my faith. Surely Sister Ruth will approve of this attitude. Maybe that is what she wants to see me do. Turn to God. I do believe that He is great and good so I will do my best to show how I feel to Sister Ruth. If that does not work I do not know what I could possibly do. I have grown a year older and I do believe that Sister Ruth will have to work very hard to break the spirit she hardened last year.

It is hard though to do in reality. I can write about doing anything. That is why I love it so. I could write about how I will grow wings and fly tomorrow, out of the school and away. I will fly tomorrow. I will fly all the way to London. The people there will greet me with banners and I will be adored. There will be songs and music and dancing all because of me. The people will shout to their neighbours to come outside and see Heather McGinley fly over their houses and wave to every one of them.

When I have flown over London, I will head South and fly over the deserts of Africa and I will live with Lions for a year, learning what they have to teach me and listening to the stories they have to tell, for you see, Lions are the most intelligent creatures on earth. So much so that they see the flaws in religion and politics and do not live by them. They live by their instincts and their love for each other. When I have learnt all that I can from them I will return to England and all the people I left behind, a grown woman. Then I will teach. I will write about everything that I know and then I will teach it to children. When a young girl does not understand, I will take her to one side and explain what it means to her and when she realises the beauty of what I tell her she will smile and thank me. That is what I will do tomorrow. I will fly.

11/10/1904

I did not fly. I will never fly for I am a caged bird. My mother has insisted that I spend my spare time away from this diary and what she calls, "The foolish pursuit of writing." She insisted it was a man's profession and that, as a woman, my place was inside at the kitchen sink and the oven. And my job is to make my husband happy. I asked if his job was to make me happy. A question which was greeted with a scowl from my mother. She told me that his happiness would make me happy.

Today I learnt to bake bread and I swear now in this journal that I will never make bread again. I will never wash dishes or dust side tables. I will not sacrifice myself to what is expected of me. I will also pay for this. I already am and I will tomorrow. I can see no other way. Sister Ruth punished me today for she tried to teach a dying language to a dying girl. When I could not answer a question she asked me in Latin I was marched out of the classroom as a man is led to the gallows. It was the march of a doomed soul.

I did not think a single thought as I walked to my unknown fate. I have learned not to by now. If you allow yourself to imagine where she is taking you then you think up something dreadful. Then when you arrive your real fate is much worse. Then your spirit is broken immediately and you have no chance of your mind surviving the trials Sister Ruth puts it through. As I came to a stop I noticed that I had descended a staircase and was in the basement. I had never seen the basement before and as I glanced at it I was glad this was the first time and I hoped that it would be the last. It was the most hideously small and damp place. The ceiling was so low that Sister Ruth had to bend slightly to get in. There were piles of old books and unused shelves arranged randomly all around the room.

I did not see how any reason for being down here

could be a pleasant one. Before I could think to ask Sister Ruth why I was in the basement, the door was slammed shut and a key was turned. I could not see. The books and shelves disappeared as I was plunged into darkness. With my sight taken from me by the darkness my other senses seemed to be on alert. I put out my hands and I felt around, breathing in the musty air. My hand fell upon something sticky. I pulled my hand away but it was stuck to me. There was something else. Something was crawling up my arm. I could feel its legs moving, tickling me. The creature reached my neck and it stopped. I raised the hand that was not in the sticky thing and felt at it. As my hand came near to the unknown monster on my neck it scurried quickly onto my face. I screamed and the creature ran down my body. I cannot be sure, but I think that it was a spider, but it must have been very large as when it sat on my face it nearly covered all of it. I was not willing now to move. I did not want to sit down in case the spider returned so I stood, in the middle of the basement for five hours. I knew that it was five, because when I had gone in it was the start of the lesson before lunch which was at eleven o'clock, and it was the end of school when I was let out, which is at four o'clock. As I stood and waited for my release I realised that I would never be released, as being locked in there, unable to move, unable to breathe without tasting foul air and unable to escape, was just how my life would be when I am married and living out the life that my mother has laid out for me. That life of baking, washing and dusting would taste the same to me as the basement did. Foul and tight. Tight like I was not able to move or escape. Like I would stand there forever, too afraid to step even a little to the side so that I could rest my feet and catch my breath. Always too afraid to open my eyes and see what the world has to offer because I know that I cannot have any of it.

Too afraid to move from the exact spot that has been assigned to me. Too afraid to stray anywhere because there are monsters everywhere, lurking, just waiting for me to fall so they can pounce on me and devour me and prove to the world that there is only one place for little girls and the women they grow into. And that place is inside. Kept inside and in the dark, away from the light of the world that would be their freedom. If only they could reach it. The light that shines down on free people in the world and lets them be the people they want to be. Writers, painters, travellers. All these people are free because they are outside and their eyes are open.

Oh how I wish I could be outside. Outside where I could sit beneath a giant oak tree and write poems about its beauty, its strength and its eternity. What a way to spend eternity that would be. To stand tall and strong for centuries not moving simply watching. Seeing. Seeing all the beauty of the world grow and die and be born again. To have birds make nests in your branches and grass grow around your roots. Having life and freedom all around you and never having to bow to anyone's wishes. Seeing the light shining, giving you life. That would be a pleasant eternity.

They will never keep me inside. I will not let them keep me away from that light. I got home today and I wrote everywhere that I could because I refuse to allow them to stop me. They cannot stop me because this is what I am meant to do. I filled my other book with poems and when that had run out I took my pen and I wrote on my wall. I wrote in large letters and clearly. I want there to be no doubt about who I am when I am dead. I want there to be no doubt that I was killed by Sister Ruth, I was killed by my Mother and my Father, I was killed by the girl in my class who did not say that Sister Ruth was wrong to do the things she did. I was killed by Sister Mary and by Joseph Walsh. I was killed by Jacob's parents and by all the men and women in this world who say that I have to stay inside. I do not like being inside.

The only times I have ever been truly happy was when I was outside with Jacob. Especially that day at the well. Not even Sister Ruth's evil deeds were enough to stop that moment from being the happiest of my life. To me that well will be a monument to my soul and my spirit. That is why I have chosen that place to see my end. I will walk to the well tomorrow morning. I will take a rope and find something heavy, I do not know what but I believe that I will find what I need. I will climb the outer wall of the well, just as I did for Sister Ruth when she wished to know the number of bricks there were, and I will let go. I will let go of all the restrictions and the limitations that have been placed on me, and I will let go of my life. For that is the only way that I will be able to fly. That is the only way that Heather McGinley, for that is my name, will be able to live in that light forever. I know that God will take me into his Heaven and he will watch with me as the world turns. Then I will see the eternity of the world the way I wish to. I will see all the glory and splendour of God's creation alongside him. When I am dead, I will tell stories to all the others who are there, and they will read my poems, and I will be free to do as I wish. When I am dead there will be no coal shed, or basement, or kitchen. There will just be me, and light, and a pen, and I will write.

Tomorrow, I will fly.

That was the end of the diary entries. Fern closed the book and sat back. It was the end, Heather was dead. She had taken her own life. A twelve year old girl had taken her own life, because she was not able to live her life the way she had wanted. That made Fern so angry but she was not able to show it. She dropped the diary on the floor and began to sob. She could not stop the tears from coming. She cried for Heather, for her life that was extinguished, for her dreams that were never realised and for the happiness she found briefly but lost all too quickly. Fern cried for a long time and she did not know why she couldn't stop. She was so angry at all the people at the school, and Heather's parents. How could they let all this happen, to a child? It was all wrong and Fern would have done anything, absolutely anything, to have gone back and helped Heather. To have taken her away from that oppression and misery. To hold her hand and reassure her. To tell her that she can be whatever she wants to be. Fern wished above all else that she could have been there on the twelfth day of October, 1904 when Heather McGinley was walking to the well and stood right in front of her. Fern wished that she could have done all the things her parents had done and encouraged her the way that her teachers had. She wished she could have told her that things would improve. That in just a few years' time, women would stand up and say no and that in the future, women would be able to write without question. But she couldn't. Heather was dead and there was nothing Fern could do. The frustration and anger at this realisation was unbearable. She broke down with a new set of tears as the hopelessness of the situation sank in.

Eventually, Fern was able to gather her thoughts. She had been on a terrifying journey with Heather, but there were still things she needed to know, questions she wanted to ask. She knew what she had to do next so she picked up the phone and rang Professor James Morgan.

Chapter Four

Morgan walked into Fern's flat. He looked older now than he had been when Fern had been to see him before and he appeared to be thinner. His glasses were no longer pressed firmly against his face. He had a look that suggested he had been anxious about something for a long time. This did nothing to reassure Fern. He took off his coat and removed his hat allowing his messy hair to tangle itself further on top of his head.

The atmosphere was awkward. Morgan knew how Fern would be feeling as he had felt the exact same way when he had read Heather's diary. Fern made them some tea and invited Morgan to sit in the arm chair while she sat on the floor. Morgan sipped his tea and looked at Fern. His eyes held a great pain. Fern could see deep inside him when he looked at her and she could tell immediately what he was going to tell her would not be easy to listen to. He put his cup down and took a deep breath. He knew he had to tell Fern the rest of the story. She had come too far to stop now. He had grown close to Heather in his research. He felt almost like a father to her. And now he had to tell this young girl in front of him about her death. He began, a slight tremble was evident in his voice,

"She died the way she had intended. There were school and police reports made and eyewitness statements taken. I read them all and between them they paint a pretty accurate picture. There are bits and pieces I had to fill in myself, read between the lines if you will. But I believe my account to be as accurate as they can be.

"Heather was seen walking towards the well with a rope tied around her waist. The girls and the nuns in the school did not think to go and find out what she was doing as they had all heard Sister Ruth tell them about Heather's odd behaviour countless times before. She walked past the well and into the field behind. She wandered around for some minutes but eventually she found what she was looking for. She stopped and some of the girls in the school watched as she tied a large rock to the end of the rope. The spectators thought that this was a very strange thing to do but they did not leave their classrooms. Heather walked back to the well and with a final glance at the school and the people that had driven her to this awful deed, she fell backwards and into the well."

Morgan was clearly disturbed by having to describe this event. Fern was not overly keen about listening to it. But after taking another sip of tea and brushing his untidy hair away from his eyes, he continued.

"A young girl by the name of Susan Cromer saw Heather fall and screamed so loudly that girls in the other classrooms heard. There was a temporary lapse in order and the girls of Saint Agnes's school ran out of their classrooms in a fit of frenzy and got all the way to the well. But they were far too late to save her. As Heather had intended, she sank right to the bottom and died.

"The girls who could see down the well saw no sign of Heather struggling. It is hard to know whether she died quickly or if she did not have the strength of spirit left inside her to carry on any kind of fight to survive. Sister Ruth pushed to the front of the crowd around the well and arrived in time to hear one of the girls shout that Heather McGinley was dead. Ruth did not speak a word. It is quite clear that many of the girls blamed Ruth for driving Heather to such madness. They had all slightly pitied Heather the previous year and to see her take her life like that. Well, the girls from her previous class could not prevent the thoughts that Sister Ruth was to blame coming to their minds. Most also wondered if their silence during Ruth's torture had played a part. Sister Mary was the only person there who managed to keep her head and she sent for the police. They arrived very quickly and managed to ascertain that Heather had killed herself. However, that is not how it was handled. Before

Heather's body was even retrieved from its watery grave, the police had filed a report that said Heather had died in a tragic accident. This of course is complete nonsense. But being a catholic school, fairly standard practice."

Morgan allowed his objective storytelling to slip slightly. But it was okay to do so as he saw that his audience agreed with him. Fern's face held a clear expression of anger on her face and Morgan read it well.

"You hate them too?" He asked Fern who said nothing but nodded slowly in response. "Don't worry. If there is one thing right about this story, it's that the bad people were punished in the end. However late in the day justice was done.

"Heather's parents were informed after the police had decided that the clear suicide was an accident. Margaret and Samuel were devastated. A policeman was sent to their home and told them that their daughter had been tragically killed when she had fallen down the well at the bottom of the field behind the school.

"The police noted down the reaction of Heather's parents. Her mother broke down and her father's usual expression of stern authority was dashed. Tears rolled down his cheek as he thanked the police man. Margaret ran upstairs and into Heather's room. It is believed this is when they saw the writing on the wall and the secret pain of their daughter for the first time. The pain they knew nothing of. They both remembered that Heather kept a journal at the same time and turned the room upside down to try and find it. When they did they sat on their daughter's bed and read every page. In a letter to her sister, Margaret spoke of feeling their guilt grow. They saw for the first time the gift that their daughter had with words and the talent she had for expressing the way she felt on paper. All the memories of their discouragement came flooding back to both of Heather's parents.

"As they read the final words their little girl had written

73

they fell into a deep depression. They saw now that the death had been no accident. Their daughter had killed herself and they had been responsible.

"Questions raced through their minds. Why had they pressured Heather into learning the ways of a housewife? Why had they listened to Sister Ruth instead of their own daughter? Why had they not seen what was happening to Heather? None of these questions could ever be answered. Retrospect is a wonderful thing and it was only with looking back that they were able to see the mistakes that they made. At the end of it all, their daughter was dead. She had taken her own life and had blamed her parents.

"It proved too much for Margaret and Samuel to take. They left the books and their daughter's other possessions with the school, as they were the only people they could think of that would have any use for them. Sister Mary took them without question as she could see it was the only thing she could do for the desperate couple. Mary eventually locked the papers away some years later and were only found when I went looking for them. After the school had changed hands and was no longer a religious facility. The last thing Margaret and Samuel wanted was to give this damning information to the police. They left their home on the day of the funeral. There is nothing I can find on Heather's parents after the sale of their home, just before Christmas, in 1904."

Fern was uneasy about this. She did not feel comfortable being in the house. The air was stale with guilt; she had not noticed it before. It was true that Heather's parents had made her life feel like Hell but Fern had been so distracted with the deeds of Sister Ruth that she had not really thought about Heather's parents. Remembering Sister Ruth suddenly brought questions to Fern's mind.

"What about Ruth? What happened to her? You said that she saw Heather after she drowned in the well but what happened to her afterwards?"

"Sister Ruth was not a very nice person. But she was still human. I understand that when you read Heather's diary it is hard to picture Ruth as a person but she was. In this period of history, women's lives were set out before them. You study English I believe. Then you must have read Plath and Woolf?"

Fern replied that she had. She had studied both writers and had felt a great unease at the stories of their lives. Morgan continued with apprehension. He felt as if he was playing devil's advocate.

"It was not impossible for women to fulfil their pre-decided fates and still become writers. However, their works tell those who read them that their lives were a constant fight for self-expression and liberty. Many died tragically. Ruth believed very strongly that she was doing the right thing for Heather. She believed that she was instilling in Heather the attitudes and manners that young girls like her should have. A vivid imagination is no friend to a girl in an Edwardian catholic school." Morgan sighed and continued.

"I am not condoning what she did but she did do those terrible things for a reason. A reason she honestly believed was rational. We know, of course, that it didn't work. Heather's imagination grew stronger and bolder with every punishment she endured. Ruth thought that she was doing the best thing, and that she was at liberty to take any means necessary to make Heather the way she was supposed to be." Fern let out an involuntary grunt of disgust at this comment. Morgan noticed, gave a wry smile and continued.

"Ruth spent a great many months without guilt. She had been told and she believed that Heather had died in a horrible accident. She knew first hand that Heather could be clumsy. She had fallen into the well before after all. But there was something playing on Sister Ruth's mind. Why had Heather been at the well in the first place? And how had she drowned? There were plenty of people around the well who could have helped her out. Over time, Ruth learned to push these doubts deep into the back of her mind. She convinced herself that it had been an accident and even if it wasn't it did not matter a great deal. Heather McGinley was dead after all. And that fact had alleviated one of Ruth's biggest headaches. She went on teaching at Saint Agnes's for the remainder of that year. But she did not return after that year was over.

"Ruth spoke to Sister Mary about one night in her home near to the school when she was disturbed by a devilish dream. She felt herself flying all over the school grounds. She saw the happy faces of the children playing beneath her in the field behind the school and in the courtyard. But she kept seeing a different face. An unhappy face was mixed in with the happy ones. This face was grey in colour and the expression was dull. The corners of the mouth were drooped down at the sides and the eyes were staring right at Ruth but they were not seeing her. Ruth saw the face several times but she did not worry about it until she saw that this face was leading her somewhere. The face appeared more and more as Ruth neared the well. Then she was no longer flying. Her feet were on the floor and she was standing at the edge of the well. She looked down into it and there was the face. It leapt out of the water, whispered, 'You killed me.' and disappeared back into the well."

Fern was disgusted at the thought that she had something in common with Sister Ruth. She desperately tried to think if there was a common reason for her and the nun to have these dreams. Then Fern became afraid. What if that common reason was revenge? What if Heather had been offended by Fern in some way? What if Heather had given Fern those dreams to make her leave the house? Fern laid away her fears as Morgan continued his story.

"These dreams went on for some time. Ruth grew slowly anxious of them and was getting suspicious about Heather's death. Ruth was a proud woman but she had confided in Sister Mary during the ordeal. Mary was horrified at the vividness of the dreams. Between them, the two women blamed them on the Devil, witchcraft and Heather herself! Even after her death, Ruth still managed to find things that she had done wrong. It never occurred to her that the dreams may have been produced through her own feelings of guilt over Heather's death.

"Mary thought it was appropriate to tell Ruth about the diaries Heather's parents had given to her before they had left. Ruth listened as Mary told her the truth about Heather's death and guilt rose slowly inside her like a hot wave of fire ebbing and flowing in her stomach. Mary saw that the story was affecting Ruth so she went to the back of her office and fetched the diary. Ruth took it eagerly and without any way of knowing what it would reveal to her.

"Ruth rushed home with the book beneath her arm and when she got home she began to read. She must have sat for the rest of that day and all night reading all the things that Heather had written about her. With this opportunity that Heather had given Ruth posthumously to see things from another person's perspective, Ruth became grieved. She was a religious woman, and although we can see that she was not a good woman, she had always believed that she had been. She went through several different possibilities. The first, as I am sure will not surprise you, was blaming Heather. Maybe she was evil and blamed Ruth for no reason other than spite.   She slowly came round to the thought that she may have been wrong. This, Sister Ruth did not take well however. Like I said she was a proud woman and she did not relish a dead student making her question her actions.

"Saint Agnes's was now closed for the summer months and Ruth spent her time at home reading the diary of the girl she had practically killed, over and over again, desperately trying to find a way of taking the blame away from herself . She did not succeed. For three whole months, Sister Ruth read the diary again and again, telling her friends in the church about the same details over and over. She was so preoccupied with it that she did not return to Saint Agnes's when she was supposed to begin teaching again. At Saint Agnes's the nuns grew worried. They had to split Ruth's class between some of the others and it was far from ideal. The classrooms were cramped with too many children and some of the girls were in years too high for their ability.

"In the end, Sister Mary went to Ruth's quarters to see what the matter was. When she went inside she was shocked by what she saw. It was a complete mess. There were books and papers scattered all around the floor. On closer inspection, Mary saw that all the books were replicas of Heather McGinley's diary. Ruth had copied Heather's words into more than one hundred separate books. That was not all. Mary looked up from the floor and noticed that the walls were also covered with writing. They were poems. Mary recognised them as the poems that Heather had written in her diary. Mary had read the book when the Heather's parents had given it to her. Now she was scared. She looked more closely at the wall and noticed that the poem Heather had written about Ruth had been copied over and over. She heard a noise. Mary turned quickly and saw that Sister Ruth was standing behind her. Her face had become thin and stretched with sleeplessness. Mary barely recognised the shadow her colleague of several years had become. Ruth's clothes were hanging off her and her mouth was set open, almost as if she was panting. She had a pen in her hand and the sharp point of it was pointing at Mary's face. She ducked out of the way as Ruth lunged at her. Ruth went lurching forward and fell onto a table in front of the fire place. Sister Mary did not hesitate. She ran as fast as she could out of the house and back to the school. She sent for the police, once again, and they hurried to the home of Sister Ruth.

"I found the police reports from the day and they went into some detail. It is fortunate for us perhaps that they were so fastidious. The police officers on that day were clearly dealing with a disturbed woman, and a nun no less. The report goes into details from all present and forms a thorough picture."

"It was not a pleasant event. The police had to capture Ruth and avoid her frenzied attacks. She did not discriminate. She flew at anyone who came near her. Eventually they caught her and took her straight to Longwood Mental Asylum. It was there that Sister Ruth lived out the rest of her sorry life. She lived to the grand age of sixty four which was quite good for a woman in her condition. She spent many long nights afraid to fall asleep, afraid that she would dream of the girl she murdered. Some days she would sit, in a kind of catatonia, staring at the wall with not a single thought in her mind. Others she would not be able to sit still. She would spend some of the day cleaning like the other patients and the rest of her time teaching the other patients about good manners and Godly living. She would threaten them as well. She would say that if they did not cooperate with her she would do what she did to all naughty little children. She would kill them."

Fern sat listening to this story with a kind of sadistic delight. She had hated Sister Ruth for the whole time that she had been reading about Heather, and she had felt physically sick at the thought that the woman had got away with what she had done. Fern closed her eyes as Morgan talked about the asylum and she pictured what it would have looked like. She saw stark white walls and cold stone floors. The doors were made out of heavy iron and were painted green, like in a prison. The patients were forced to walk around in threadbare gowns with nothing on their feet. The cold floor punishing them as they walked from room to room. The beds were some kind of metal it was hard to tell which as they were covered with rust. The mattresses that had been placed on the rusty beds were thin, hard and topped with a pillow that was little more than a white cotton case with a handful of feathers inside. Each bed was adorned with one harsh grey blanket that kept no cold out in the winter and trapped the heat in the summer. The communal toilets were cleaned religiously by the patients and the stink of carbolic soap was a permanent feature. The nurses took turns to assist anyone who needed help in them as the smell was strong enough to turn their stomachs.

There was one communal room designated for socialising. Fern imagined this was where Ruth 'taught' the patients. There were two brown sofas and a small bookshelf that had three books placed on the shelves.

The sofas were as uncomfortable as the springs beneath them had broken before they had even been given to the asylum. Fern also saw Sister Ruth. She was sitting at the end of one of the sofas and staring at the white wall. Fern heard Morgan say that Ruth had no thoughts in her head, but Fern knew that was not true. Ruth was thinking all right. There was one thought that was in her head. It was the thought that is always in her head. It is the thought of that face. The dead face of the little girl she had killed. And it haunted her. Fern knew it. She didn't know how but she knew. Sister Ruth would sit there, staring, seeing nothing but the dead face of Heather McGinley staring back at her, the only thoughts passing through her mind were ones of guilt and confusion and pain. How could a woman who believed so strongly that she was a servant of God, cope with the knowledge that she helped a young girl on her way to taking her own life?

Fern allowed this fantasy to dwell a little in her mind. She pictured Ruth replaying the day Heather died over and over in her mind, asking herself if she could have been responsible. Believing herself incapable of acts that would lead to a most terrible sin. Growing steadily more and more confused. Insanity sucking out reason and rationality from her mind until she was no more than a shell of a human being. Fern smiled a guilty smile.

Fern was brought back to reality when Morgan finished telling her of the fate of Sister Ruth. Despite the hatred both these people had for the nun, neither of them was happy about this outcome. Fern had been imagining the awful environment in which Ruth had spent the last years of her life and she had smiled. But now she was thinking how terrible it was. If she had just been willing to let Heather do what she wanted with her life. If all these people had listened to that one young girl, none of this needless pain would have occurred. This thought made Fern feel sick again. She was glad that Ruth was made to suffer but she only suffered that insanity because of the pain she caused Heather. And Fern would have preferred it if none of that had happened at all.

Morgan was not yet ready to leave. He had more to tell Fern about the consequences of Heather's death and the insanity of Sister Ruth.

"The school was in an inevitable state of turmoil after these events had unfolded. There was a great feeling of guilt among the students in Heather's class and a number of the nuns decided that it was a good time to go on missionary duty. The school was low on teachers and several nuns came and went in response to the crisis at Saint Agnes's. But there was a bigger problem than the lack of teachers. After the funeral of Heather, many of the girls had requested to Sister Mary that the well be covered over permanently and kept as a memorial to her. Mary was reluctant to cover over the well but she consented because of safety reasons. The last thing that Saint Agnes's needed at that time was another accident. So the well was covered and was, unofficially, turned into a memorial for Heather.

None of the girls had been her friend but every last one of her classmates had felt the blow of the cane when Sister Ruth had struck her. Fear had been the only thing that had kept the girls from becoming Heather's friends. Now, they all felt like they were to blame for Heather's death. Not a single one of them had believed Sister Mary when she had told them it had been an accident. Susan Cromer had told her fellow students what she had seen, even though the police and Sister Mary had told her not to. Every day there were fresh flowers placed on the well. At first they were placed there by many of the students, even some of the teachers. After a while the number of flowers diminished as the students began to forget Heather McGinley but the flowers were still put there by a few of Heather's old classmates. Susan Cromer was among this number. I do not believe that Miss Cromer ever forgot Heather. It is not clear from what I have read but I believe she continued to place a posy of flowers on Heather's well once a year for the rest of her life, on the twelfth of October.

"The school was going quickly downhill. They had lost the trust of the church and funding was not forthcoming. The nuns at Saint Agnes's were understandably distressed, most of them put in for transfers or asked to leave teaching altogether and the school was closed in 1906. By this time, the only nun who had been there when Heather had died was Sister Mary.

"The girls were all sent to different schools around the area. I know that it is hard for you to see any good come out of this situation, Fern. But look at the girls she was at school with. They have learnt from this and my studies have led me to discover that some of them, albeit a very small number, went on to become something worthwhile. One of them even got involved in the Suffragette movement."

Fern was comforted only a little by this news. She had hoped that the school had closed and she also was glad that the girls learnt something positive from their time at Saint Agnes's. But there was still one end that Morgan had not tied up.

"What about Jacob? Heather said he was the only one who understood her. What happened to him?"

Morgan took another deep breath. He found Jacob's story very distressing. Morgan looked at Fern. The anticipation and willingness to throw herself into this story made Morgan believe she would do something with this information. He did not know what exactly, but something was telling him as he looked into her eyes that it was more than worth his while to continue telling this story to Fern. Morgan gathered his thoughts and began to tell Fern of Jacob's fate.

"You are right. Jacob was the only person in Heather's life that she did not blame for her death. It just so happened that Jacob was very similar to Heather in many ways. He laughed at what she found funny and cried when she felt pain, and he also kept a diary. I did not bring it for you because it is very hard to read his hand writing but I will tell you the important things that he wrote about Heather if you wish."

Fern nodded once again, she did not feel she should speak in case she disrupted Morgan's train of thought. She settled down on the floor to listen to Morgan once more.

"Jacob was a very intelligent young man. The reasons that he got caned at his school were because he tended to answer back and correct the teachers on their grammar. He did not want to be a writer though. He wanted to be a politician and he wrote at great length about what he would do if he were to become Prime Minister of England. Of course, he never made it that far, but he did have some good ideas. Many of these were clearly because of Heather. His longing to close Catholic schools and ban the cane were stronger than any other desire he had to change rules and laws after Heather's death.

"He loved Heather deeply. Their friendship was purely platonic and without either party wishing it to be any more. They were deeply frustrated however. They understood each other in a way that I find hard to understand. Both of them were trapped, but in different ways. Heather was trapped because she was a woman but Jacob was trapped by his intellect and his parents' lack of wealth. He was not able to gain all the information he wanted because his parents could not afford to send him to a better school. The teacher that taught him during Heather's first year with Ruth simply labelled him as an attention seeker. I shudder to think what lessons Jacob actually learnt at school. Every time he spoke he would be punished with physical pain. We are lucky that he had an unbreakable spirit. He lived a long and happy life. We know that he never allowed his grief for Heather to take over his years on this earth. He must have found a way of venting his anger over the tragedy. However, I have regretfully been unable to find what that method was." Morgan took a fresh sip of tea and went on,

"He hated the first teacher who taught him. He was called Mr Peters and he was as cruel as Sister Ruth. He even wrote that he suspected they were in competition with each other to see which one could be the most evil. He was determined to throw Jacob out of the school at one point. He went to the Head Master several times during that first year requesting that Jacob be removed. Thankfully, Jacob never knew of this and the Head Master took no notice. If Jacob had known I am sure he would only have made things worse for himself. The Head Master believed that if a boy was too ill behaved for their school then no other school would dare take him. He also believed that if there was any place on earth that could rehabilitate Jacob it was at Wainwright School For Boys. Mr Peters could not argue with this odd kind of flattery. The Head Master had more or less told him that if he could not set Jacob right then he wasn't fit to teach at Wainwright's. Peter was lucky that Jacob did not cause too much trouble. His friendship with Heather had calmed him down somewhat, although he did still get the occasional detention. Both Jacob and Peter breathed a sigh of relief when their year together was over and Jacob was moved onto a new class.

"Jacob was a lot less bothered by the punishments he received than Heather was. He knew that once he left the school he could escape and become the man he wanted to be and this more than likely saved his life. He used to wander after school had finished and think about what his life would be like after he had left school. He decided, three weeks into the second year of his education at Wainwrights that he would leave the town of his birth and move to London. Once there, he would become the Prime Minister and send for Heather. He was going to tell Heather this on the day that she died.

"Jacob heard about the death in the worst way imaginable. He was walking home, the way he usually did, so that he could tell Heather of his plan. He was late to meet her that day because he had been given lines to write for being insolent again and he was worried that she would not have waited for him. When he arrived at the corner of Holly Street, which is where they usually met, she was not there so he sat on a wall and waited. He was presuming that she had been kept behind to write lines as he had or some such punishment. He did not wait long before he saw three girls from Saint Agnes's walking down the street towards him. They were upset and he was bored with waiting, so he asked what was wrong. They told him that a girl had fallen down the well and drowned.

This was all they managed to get out before Jacob ran off towards Saint Agnes's. He knew. He knew that the dead girl was Heather. He ran all the way to the school. He burst through the heavy doors as if there were made out of air and ran down the corridor. He passed several nuns on the way but they did not question his presence. It was not the day for it. He reached the end of the corridor and noticed that the door to his right was open, it led to the field. He turned quickly and sprinted across the grass to the well. He saw his uncle and some policemen at the side of it. They were trying to pull something out but it was proving to be quite heavy. For a minute, Jacob believed it wasn't Heather. It couldn't have been because she was a small girl who he could have easily pulled out.

His pace slowed with this thought and he stopped a few feet from the well. The men had succeeded in their task and in one final quick movement; the soaking wet body of Heather McGinley was pulled from the well. He saw her face. It was his friend. He would recognise her anywhere but she was not the same. She never would be alive in his mind again. Her face was contorted, permanently set in an expression of fear and desperation. Her mouth was set open and it seemed to have turned black. Her once pink skin had turned grey and she did not look like a twelve year old girl. If her size had not given her away, you would not believe that she was a child. Jacob stood, staring at the dead eyes that were staring back at him. That is what made him cry and that is what haunted his dreams for the rest of his life. That those eyes, those beautiful blue eyes that had once looked at him with such fondness and playfulness and joy were now staring at him with nothing. There was nothing behind those eyes anymore when once there had been everything.

A policeman leant down and closed her eyes. She was dead and Jacob knew it. He broke down and his uncle noticed him for the first time. He ran over to his devastated nephew and took him home. Jacob was never the same again. He had lost something more than a friend that day. He had lost his hope. Whenever, he had felt that there was no way out, Heather had been there with a smile and a laugh. He remembered the day they had argued about the clouds and what they looked like for the rest of his life. He had lost his dream that day. His dream of them being together for ever. He had not merely wanted Heather to go with him he had needed her to go. He realised as he sat at home that night that he was alone. He had experienced a year of perfect friendship. It was too short a time. He did not understand how God or whoever it was controlling fate could allow such an ideal partnership to be torn apart so soon. And so easily. They had been almost the same person at times, as if they had merely been placed into two different bodies. Like Heather he had no real friends at his school and his parents were not interested. He had four older brothers and his parents were often more interested in their lives than his.

"On the day of the funeral, Jacob sat at the back of the church and was not able to watch her casket be lowered into the ground. He couldn't. It made it all so final. All the time he had been waiting for her to be buried, there was a small part of Jacob that was convinced she would just sit up and laugh and tell him it was all a big joke. When she was buried that last bit of hope inside Jacob's heart was buried with her. After the service, he stayed and watched as the groundskeeper covered the coffin with soil. It took them several long hours, and when they finished they remarked on the tragedy of losing one so young and they left. Jacob stood over the grave. He stared at the headstone that read,

> Here lies the body of Heather McGinley.
> Who died at age twelve on 12/10/1904.
> It is a great loss to all and a tragic death
> of a young girl. She is with God now.

He found it hard to read the words as he had not yet allowed himself to believe that she was gone. When you want something badly enough you persuade yourself that you can have it. I suppose that it works the other way around as well. Jacob did not want his friend to be dead. She was all alone. How would she cope with being all alone? He had promised that he would always be with her. He did not allow himself to accept that she was gone. But she was. His denial found no way around Heather being buried. He was looking at her grave, no one else's, hers. He felt a single tear roll down his face as he realised that she had gone. She was gone forever and nothing he could do would change that. He hated the finality of it. He hated that this was it. Like a line had been drawn under Heather's life. The frustration at these thoughts tired Jacob. He felt almost as if he couldn't think any more. A pain came to his stomach. It ached there for many years and it came back to him from time to time for the rest of his life.

"He thought about Heather a lot and his diary is full of his pain at losing her. He muddled through the remainder of his childhood with a great depression hanging over his head. He was never quite able to come to terms with the untimely death of his friend and confidant. All the great memories of her haunted him for the rest of his life. He took to looking skyward to gaze at the clouds and see if he could see one that looked like her. He never did but he never stopped believing that when he saw clouds that looked like rabbits, that was Heather having a laugh at his expense.

"He remembered her smile throughout his journal. Her smile would not fade for him. She would always be smiling in Jacob's memory. Except when he dreamt of the day she died. That was the only time her smile went, when he saw her face as she was pulled from the well. He tried harder at keeping that image out of his mind than he did at anything in his life.

"I was fortunate to get hold of this diary. Jacob was married, to a wonderful woman called Jemima. They had five children. One girl and four boys. The girl was called Heather and on the day that Jacob died, he gave his diary to his daughter and asked her to read it. She did and she kept it. It was from her that I got the diary. She too was in love with her name sake and was more than willing to share her story with me. She told me that her father had loved her mother very much but he was always thinking of Heather. Her mother consented to naming their daughter Heather because she understood that it meant so much to him. I took the book while thanking her greatly."

Fern was amazed. She had not realised from Heather's diary that Jacob had loved Heather so much. His story was so tragic and Fern felt for him so much. He was clearly a very good person who cared for Heather more than she knew. If only she did know. That could have saved her. If someone believes that there is one person who loves them and they love that person back, there is always something to live for. Fern was finding it hard not to share Jacob's grief. The boy can't have been older than thirteen when Heather died Fern could not even comprehend what it must have been like to carry grief like that for all those years.

Fern sat and did not speak to Morgan for what seemed like hours. He did not expect her to. He left her to think while he went into Fern's bedroom to take a look at the writing on the wall. He had never seen inside Heather's house before and he was in awe of what she had written. He reminded himself that she had been twelve but it was hard for him to believe. He left the room and returned to the living room. Fern was still taking in what he had told her so he decided that he should leave. He told Fern to contact him if she needed any more information on Heather McGinley or the people around her. Fern acknowledged what he had said and helped him gather the papers he had lent her. She showed him out of her home and went back into the living room. It was so much to take in.

Morgan had taken all the books away so she had nothing to remind her of the story. Fern decided she had to have something for reference. She needed to have a record of all the things she had learnt tonight and over the last few days. She took out a note book and began to write the story down. She did not want to forget a single thing that she had found out that day, she had gone on a journey. She had discovered that she was lucky she could do what she wanted with her life. If the story of Heather McGinley had taught her nothing else, it had taught her that she shouldn't take anything for granted. So Fern sat down and she began to write.

Fern wrote a brief account of Heather McGinley's life.

She wrote it for no other person than herself and she wrote it fast. By the time she had finished it was past midnight. She sat in the living room of her one person flat and noticed for the first time in two days that she was hungry. She had snacked through the last few days but she hadn't eaten a proper meal.

Fern walked into the kitchen and looked at the room in a different way. She had never seen it as something to fear before. But that is how Heather had seen it. The injustice of the expectations on women of that time, of all time, hit Fern as she stared at the kitchen. The relief that she did not have to spend her life here grew. As did her desire to fulfil her own dream and become a writer. Fern put a microwave meal in to cook and sat down, listening for the beep that would tell her she could eat. She wondered if Heather's life would have been different if she had had microwaves and dishwashers and all the home comforts that Fern had. Would that have stopped her from being so scared of being a wife and staying inside? Fern heard the beep and sat down with her meal.

She ate thinking about Heather. Fern now had an understanding that she did not have before. She had read poems and books by oppressed women before, but she had never realised that there were so many that had been so trapped by society that they had never even got a chance to be published. When she thought about it, it seems quite obvious that must have happened. Fern turned on the television and watched a show about the Second World War without listening to a word that was said. Fern had learnt from the story of Heather. She knew now that it was not only a privilege to be able to write, but she now felt a certain level of duty. She felt like she had to. All her dreams about becoming a writer now seemed more like plans to be one. Fern decided there and then that she would do whatever she could to fulfil that dream.

But there was still something that was playing on Fern's

mind. It was clear that Heather had made Fern notice her and find out about her life. But why? There must have been a reason? Mustn't there?

The television went off. Fern was deep in thought but this time she noticed. She looked to see if she had been sitting on the remote control but it was on the top of the TV. As Fern rose to turn it back on some force pushed her back down into the chair. It was so strong. Fern tried to stand but was being held in the seat. She felt fear rise quickly within her. She tried again but she could not get up from the chair. She listened as sounds of breaking glass were heard coming from the kitchen; it was as though they were being picked up and thrown. Fern did not like this at all. None of her glasses or plates or bowls were out. They were all in the cupboards. Fern tried to turn round in the chair but she could not move any part of her body. A freezing cold gust of air came surging past her. It was so cold that it made Fern shudder and her breath was visible in the air.

Her breath was pumping in and out of her as she desperately tried to see what was going on. She did not understand, this did not feel like Heather. The TV began to rock then it went smashing onto the floor. Fern let out a scream but it was inaudible. Every door in the flat was being opened and slammed shut. There were two pictures hung on the wall and they went flying across the room and smashed into each other, falling right in front of Fern. Shards of glass went splintering across the room. Fern closed her eyes but she could not move any other part of her body. She opened her eyes again to vainly try and comprehend what was happening to her. The wallpaper fell from the walls as if it was too heavy to be held up. The small table that the TV had been resting on was upturned and the legs were bent out of shape.

Just as Fern was starting to think clearly, pots and pans and the glasses that weren't already broken came flying through into the living room. They all smashed on the wall and Fern screamed as a piece of glass sliced into the side of her face. The pain was excruciating and when Fern let out her yell of hurt, the ghost stopped its mischief. Fern was released and she fell from the chair to the floor putting her shaking hands tentatively to her wound. Her fingers found a shard of glass protruding from her cheek. She moved her fingers either side to see if she could remove it but she was hit with a fresh wave of pain through her face. Fern left the glass where it was and tried to move around the room. She did not know where she should go or what she should do but she had to do something.

The air was freezing all around Fern now, her breath gasping clouds of vapour in quick succession. She was sobbing. It was not because of the pain, it was out of frustration. For some months now, Fern did not even know how long it had been, the spirit of Heather McGinley had been haunting her day and night, filling her head with horrendous dreams of the death and the pain and the misery of a little girl. She was miles away from home and the house she was living in had been turned upside down by this ghostly presence. Fern had fallen way behind in her studies and as she sat sobbing in the wake of Heather's latest fit of despair Fern realised that she would have to do the year all over again. This thought angered her. Fern stood, looked up to the ceiling as she did not know where to look to address Heather and said,

"You have taken this far enough Heather McGinley!" She shouted with desperation in her voice.

"You have destroyed my home. You have turned my life upside down. You have made me a prisoner in my own home. What the Hell is it that you want? Why do you give me those dreams? What is it that I can do? What do you want from me?!"

With these questions hanging in the air Heather unleashed a whirlwind in Fern's living room. The air was going round the room with Fern in the middle of it all. The wind got faster and faster and colder and colder. Fern dropped to the floor and covered her face as best she could. The sound was deafening. It was a hurricane in her ears. Fern tried to block it out but it was too loud. She struggled against the tumult in the room, unsure of where she was even in this all too familiar room. She sat shivering and wishing that this nightmare would just end. The winds grew fiercer and colder. Fern screwed herself up as much a possible on the floor of her flat. The winds can't have been raging for ten minutes but it felt like ten hours to Fern. Then it stopped. The winds ceased and the air went warm again.

Fern sat up. She noticed the pain in her cheek once more and winced. She stood and looked around the room. She did not know whether to be glad at what she saw or not. The television was back on the table, which had straight legs once more. The pictures were back on the wall and the wallpaper was put back the way it had been. All the broken dishes and glasses were back in the kitchen. There was only one thing that told Fern that Heather was still around. The top corner of one of the pieces of wall paper was hanging down. Fern could see that there was something written beneath it but she could not see what. She pulled the armchair up to the wall and climbed on to it. She took hold of the wall paper and pulled. There was writing on the wall. It had not been there when Heather had pulled the paper off a moment ago. It was a single word, written in high, black letters. The word was,

'Help'

Fern was not sure what she could do, she was not even sure why Heather needed her help. Then she knew. A rush of cold air took her again. It rushed past her, then it started to move around her, over her, under her. Fern was beginning to think this felt really bad when the air lifted her off her feet and threw her across the room. She smashed into the wall with great force and felt her arm break at the elbow. Pain shot once more through her body. Fern realised all at once why Heather was in need of her help. She knew why Heather had made her see all those awful things. Heather needed Fern's help because she was not alone. All those awful things that were happening to Heather that Fern saw in her dreams were shown to her because they weren't over. Heather was not the only spirit in the house.

The force of whatever had blown Fern through the air had been strong. Fern had broken her arm but she had also bashed her head pretty hard. She stayed conscious just long enough to realise Sister Ruth must be the other ghost in the flat but she soon fell into a dark pit of unconsciousness.

This dream was not like the others. Fern was herself in this one. She was not inside Heather like before. She was in the halls of Saint Agnes's School for Girls and there were hundreds of girls around her. Not a single one of them noticed her, no one could see her. Fern walked down the corridor past familiar looking classrooms. Fern had been here before but this time it felt different. She knew she was heading somewhere but she did not know exactly where. The corridor was longer than it had been in her previous dreams but she reached the room that she was supposed to go into. She knew when she saw the door that she was meant to go in, it was as though she had been through it a thousand times before. She entered the room and saw Sister Ruth talking to her class. There were Latin phrases on the board and Sister Ruth was getting irate about something.

Her ugly face was twisted with disgust and her cold grey eyes were staring straight at one of the girls. Her eyes were unblinking as she yelled words Fern could not hear at one of her students. Fern followed Sister Ruth's eye line and saw that Heather was standing up at her desk. She was looking directly at Fern. Her eyes were in stark contrast to Ruth's. They were a deep dark shade of blue and they were looking at Fern with a sense of longing. It was as though she wanted something from her but could not say what it was. Sister Ruth was barely audible at this point but Fern could tell that she was demanding that Heather look at her and answer the question she had been asked. But Heather did not look at Sister Ruth. She was staring at Fern and whispering something. But Fern could not hear what she was saying. Fern was growing anxious. She could hear Sister Ruth's demands growing louder and louder, drowning out Heather as she tried to speak to Fern so she could hear. Fern was upset. She looked at Sister Ruth and she looked at Heather. It was all so loud now. She couldn't hear Heather. Fern tried to open her mouth and shout to Heather that she couldn't hear but no sound came out. She did not know what Heather wanted to say but she knew that she had to hear it. Suddenly, Fern let out a scream. It was so loud that it made Heather cover her ears. Sister Ruth turned and looked at Fern.

"You will never kill me."

Fern looked at Sister Ruth as she said this to her and the face she saw was older than it had been. The nun's skin was paler and creased so much it was hard to tell that it was the same woman. Fern was startled by the look of this face, this clearly insane face. The eyes were staring with an intent that could not be known by Fern. Ruth's expression was one of hatred and malcontent. Fern knew she must get away from that face. That hideous face, embittered with years of malice. Heather was next to Fern now,

"Come with me."

Fern and Heather raced down the corridor together the bellowing sound of Sister Ruth was following them. Fern could not hear her and she did not want to. She just ran with Heather by her side. She did not ever want to stop. She wanted to run with Heather until they were a hundred miles away from this place. Fern wanted more than anything to take Heather away from this school. As they reached the end they turned right. They were running outside and before Fern could realise where they were going they were at the well. Fern turned to Heather but she wasn't there. Fern panicked. Where had she gone? She had been there a second ago and now she couldn't see her. Fern saw the well and she knew that she must take one final look down that well if she wanted to help Heather. She peered over the edge. She could feel prickles down the back of her neck as her hairs there stood on end.

She had seen this once before and she did not want to see it again. Just as she was about to step back a hand grabbed her neck. It was Sister Ruth. Fern saw an evil flash in the eyes of the nun and then she was pushed. Fern fell into the deep, murky waters of the well but she was not frightened. She did not know how it was possible but she wasn't drowning. Heather's face was suddenly before hers. The face of a twelve year old girl. An alive face. She smiled at Fern and she suddenly saw all the beauty that Jacob had seen. Her smile was infectious and Fern smiled back at her. The water began to ripple and Fern looked up to see if Sister Ruth was coming after them. She wasn't. Fern looked back at Heather and saw the dead face looking straight at her,

"Get her out. I cannot be free if she is not cast out."

Fern woke up. Her arm was numb but the wound in her face was aching badly. But she knew what she had to do. Summoning strength from deep down Fern stood tall and defiant in the middle of the room.

"Heather, if you can hear me, I stand with you. I stand with you against Sister Ruth. I hear your story, your words and I believe you. I am with you. I will live your dream for you, I will write to the end of my days and I will honour your memory as I do it. I won't forget you."

A soft rush of cold air sent a shiver down the left hand side of Fern's body and she turned her head in that direction. Standing beside her was the wispy likeness of Heather. Her eyes looked up and met Fern's. A sense of defiance shone from them and Fern gained confidence that what was about to happen would work. It had to work.

The girls both turned towards the other side of the room.

Fern didn't know if Sister Ruth was there but Heather seemed to. Fern felt a cold, firm but oddly unsubstantial grip on her left hand and she took a step forward with the ghost of Heather. The cold, gushing air moved around them. Ruth was still here. Freezing the air around them.

Heather spoke. Goosebumps rose all over Fern's body but she stood firm and gripped Heather's hand as tightly as she could.

"Sister Ruth, you spent too long torturing me. No one heard my cries, no one took my side. The whole world was against me and I had nowhere to turn. Until now, now I have a friend who has power over you, a friend who can help me get you away for good. Get out of my house, Sister. Get out. Get. Out!"

There was a massive blast of warm air that was strong enough to blow the already weakened Fern to the floor. Once again there was a deafening noise. Although this time it sounded more like a roar. A sudden shot of blindingly bright light came bursting into the room. Fern was thrown backwards and as she lay on the floor many memories came back to her. Heather's desperation and dreams. Ruth's cruelty. Jacob's love for his friend. The hopelessness, the despair. Then a different feeling came over Fern. Her eyes were shut but she saw a smile. A smile that seemed glad and happy and full of hope. It was not a smile Fern had seen on Heather's face before. It was heavenly. Fern felt a great satisfaction. She had helped Heather. This girl who had suffered. This girl who had taught her so much and shown her what is important. Fern had felt indebted to Heather, but she realised, as she watched that smile disappear into a cool and welcoming light, that she had done what Heather had wanted her to do. She had helped to release her. She had set her free. And that is all Heather had ever wanted.

Heather's ghost faded slowly, she never took her eyes of Fern and Fern sat staring at this girl who had bewitched her for so long. The form of this girl, 100 years dead disappeared and Fern sobbed. Deep, uncontrollable sobs that came from the very bottom of her soul.

Fern stood up slowly and took stock of the room, it would take a lot to get it fixed up but that didn't bother her, it was almost like it was necessary to bring the house back to life again after so much pain. Fern took a moment to take it all in. The house felt different now, she no longer felt a sense of disease. The house was at rest. . The house was quiet.

Chapter Five
Twenty Years Later.

Fern woke up at seven in the morning, as she almost always did these days, and turned over to look at her husband. He always looked peaceful she thought, when he was sleeping. Fern turned back over and got out of bed trying hard not to wake him. He could stay asleep a little longer. She walked into the bathroom and climbed into the shower. As she massaged shampoo into her hair she thought about her day ahead. The kids needed to be ready for school before she could relax with a hot cup of tea while her husband got his breakfast. He always left his breakfast until the kids had left because he enjoyed the peace and quiet. He much preferred eating in silence first thing in the morning.

After her leisurely morning she would have to start some work. Being self-employed had its advantages, she thought, if it meant she did not have to start work until after lunch. Although she couldn't get away with that every day. She left the bathroom and went back into the bedroom where her husband was still sleeping. She had so much love for him. She would have been content just staying in bed with him for the rest of the day, but a soft rumble in her stomach told her it was breakfast time.

Slipping on her dressing gown she walked out of the bedroom and headed to the stairs. She could hear what sounded like a war breaking out downstairs so she knew that the kids must be up already. Before she walked down the staircase to help Ann, the nanny, bring peace to the kitchen fight that broke out most mornings, she stopped to look at something. Fern loved the way she felt just after she woke up. She had spent much of her younger days sleeping in but had found in later life that the mood she woke up early in the morning was pleasantly serene.

Life went at a much slower pace first thing. A pace she could deal with. She looked at her bookcase and a smile stretched her mouth into a crescent. She was looking at nine books. All hardbacks, all first editions, all written by her. She had been first published when she was twenty-seven with a fiction book about a nine year old girl with Tourette's. The book was two hundred pages of the tear jerking incidents that made this girl's life difficult but ended with a positive twist that Fern hoped her readers would find inspiring. The girl grew up and became an author. Fern liked writing about authors. She particularly liked writing about children who wanted to be writers and women who had obstacles put in their way, preventing their expression. She had not forgotten why that was.

She descended the staircase and entered the kitchen. Fern saw Ann desperately trying to stop her two sons, Edward and Michael from fighting. It had something to do with who would eat the final chocolate finger. Fern settled the argument in her usual diplomatic way.

"That was delicious." She exclaimed, licking her lips. Edward and Michael looked at her. They were ten and twelve years old. Plenty old enough to know that wasn't fair. They started to shout at their mother but Fern just laughed, trying not to spit biscuit crumbs all over the floor. Ann stopped laughing at them all long enough to tell them that she had finished preparing their breakfast. Fern thought about her husband as she ate, wondering when he would decide to get up, and if it would be in time to see the boys off to school. She always looked forward to their mornings together. It was the only time they got to be alone. They would talk every morning about the boys, or work, or where they plan to go on holiday.

Fern married Andrew when she was twenty five. He had studied psychology at university and the two of them saw the world from entirely differing perspectives. But it worked, and they loved each other. They both had a mutual love of writing, hers was for creativity and his for science. But it was a bonding characteristic that held them together and each inspired the other.

The ceremony was a small one, just a handful of family and friends. Fern had wanted to elope but Andrew insisted on a ceremony. She was glad he did, it was a lovely day with those closest to them and she had never felt so happy. The best part for Fern though was the next day. They decided to set off straight away for a honeymoon in Scotland and the drive up there gave them chance to talk and digest the day before.

They spoke about things they had never discussed before. Fern wondered how long that could go on for, how long is it before a couple know each other completely? The conversation turned to their student days. Andrew confessed to not living the stereotypical student life. He was a bit too studious to spend all his time drinking. But he had enjoyed it nonetheless.

When it was Fern's turn to talk the atmosphere changed. There was only one part of her university experience that she could think of in that moment.

Andrew asked her what her university life had been like, what had inspired her to become a writer and a whole host of other questions that she did not feel ready to answer. Fern tried to put him off but Andrew persisted and she reluctantly told him the whole story. She trod carefully around the ghost parts and tried harder than ever to excuse how she had basically thrown away her second year of university to research a girl who died one hundred years ago.

Andrew sat and listened intently as the story unfolded, the dreams, the writing on the wall, the diary, the poems. Eventually, when Fern had finished the entire harrowing tale, she sighed and asked her new husband not to make fun of her. His response was not what she expected.

He launched himself into a detailed and complicated psychological explanation for the whole thing. He hypothesised that Heather had been a creation of Fern's stress of living by herself for the first time and her desire to be a writer. He went on for many minutes about the dreams and the hallucinations being resultant of a combination of her anxiety and powerful imagination. At the end of this analysis, Fern was left stunned. Then she heard Andrew burst out laughing.

"Sorry, Fern. I couldn't resist. But I do have a question. You have a million great ideas that you turn into fantastic stories. But you have a readymade book right there. Why have you never written it?"

Mixed in with her feelings of annoyance over the joke, Fern was left asking herself why she never had written a book about Heather. It was true that she had thought about it. How could she not have? It was an important part of her life and it changed her profoundly. Before Heather, Fern had only wanted to be a writer. Afterwards she had needed to be one. Almost every time she had started a new book the fleeting idea of writing about Heather and Jacob and Sister Ruth rushed through her mind but she always suppressed it. Was it really her place to tell this story?

Chapter Six

   After breakfast the family parted company to do their individual things. The boys were sent off to school. Driven by the irrepressible Ann. Sometimes, Fern wondered how she would cope without her. Andrew came downstairs and the couple were left by themselves for an hour while Ann was out and they decided to have their annual discussion about their next projects. This was usually an exciting time for Fern but this year she didn't have any ideas. She usually spoke to Andrew so he could help her pick out an idea out of the many she had for her next book. But this year she didn't even have one. Andrew specialised in abnormal psychology and he had wanted to look into psychopathic behaviour for some time. He now had enough time and money to do it. He warned Fern that the study would no doubt be harrowing but it would be rewarding as it was a dream of his to publish theories on the psychology of psychopathy.

   Fern did not know what she was going to do. She threw a few ideas around, one about a woman who was married to a man who abused her, forcing her to stay at home and not have a job of her own but who felt an irrepressible desire to leave and pursue her dream of acting on the stage. Another idea was a teenager who was counting down the days until she left the care system but was terrified about what might be waiting for her outside of it, but Fern felt there was no magic in these ideas. Nothing grabbed her and took her along a road to new and exciting ideas.

   "I know exactly what I am going to do."
Fern said with so much self-confidence Andrew felt a little uneasy with what his wife was going to say next. She did have a tendency of having wild ideas that never turned out well.

   "I will write a children's book."
   Andrew breathed a sigh of relief.

"It will be about lions. Lions that can talk. There will be a whole pride of them. An old male, who is the leader of the pride, but is looking for a young cub to take over his duties when he dies. There will be two male cubs and two female ones. The story will be about all the adventures they get into. There will be highs and lows but in the end they will all learn a valuable lesson."

"And what will that valuable lesson be exactly?" Andrew asked with bewilderment.

"That men and women are equal of course!"

"But of course!" Andrew knew the answer she would give. His wife had been highly praised by modern feminists for her work. All of her nine published books had included strong feminist themes. Fern was never very comfortable with being called a feminist, she didn't really know what it meant these days but she took on the title because it gave her a very large audience of similarly minded women who seemed to agree with her sentiments.

It was also a very satisfying audience. Fern received letters almost every day from women who felt touched by her stories. Fern found those letters much more satisfying than the ones from her publisher that informed how many copies she had sold. Fern would much rather sell one book to one woman and change her life for the better, than sell a million books to a million people who didn't understand her point.

Fern spent the rest of that day planning her children's book. But there was something playing on her mind. She knew that this idea had come from somewhere in her memory but she did know not where. It had not been an idea that she had long ago. She knew that because she had never even thought about writing a book for children before. She tried to forget it, but the thought that she could be plagiarising someone weighed too heavily on her mind and she was unable to work on it for long.

She walked back upstairs and looked at her books. Her name stood out clearly on each. She ran her finger along the spines, feeling the raised letters of her name. Even though she was standing looking at them, she still did not quite believe that she was a full-time writer. It had taken a long time. She had not been able to live off the profits from the first book and even though she ended up with a two book deal from her publisher she still had to work full-time alongside it. Finding time to edit was sometimes too much and she often found herself booking leave so she could hide away at home and get some work done.

Maybe she would wake up soon and be back at the flat she lived in as a student. She would wake and the whole thing, her whole life would have been a dream. No Heather, no Sister Ruth, no Andrew. This was not a pleasant thought, but Fern kicked around the idea of writing a story about a woman who wakes to find her life is not what she thought it was. Her husband didn't recognise her, her children didn't know who she was. And a strange woman claimed to be her sister. That could work.

Fern picked up her third book. It was her favourite. It was about a young girl who had been badly abused by the carers in the orphanage she had grown up in. When she grew up she had become a journalist. She used her skills and contacts to expose the men and women who had tortured her as a child.

Fern flicked mindlessly through the pages. Why could she not think of another story that she liked? She had always had so many but sometimes she could just tell they wouldn't work out for a full length book. If only she could remember where she had got the idea about the lions. She put the book carefully back on the shelf and went downstairs. As she passed a mirror halfway down the small scar on her cheek caught her eye but she quickly turned away.

"I'm not writing about that."

She muttered quickly to herself as she descended the rest of the stairs.

The doorbell rang. Fern could hear her husband on the

105

phone in the kitchen and she knew that Ann wouldn't be back yet so she went to answer it. Still with the thoughts of her children's book on her mind. When she opened the door there was a very old lady standing on the door step, stooped over and dressed in a long brown rain coat.

"Can I come in dear? I could do with a sit down."

The old lady walked into the house without waiting for a response. Fern was perplexed but she allowed her to enter. She didn't look much like a threat. Fern followed the old lady into the living room where they both sat down facing each other.

Fern found it difficult to guess her age. From the way she looked she must have been over eighty but she moved with an unexpected slow grace. The old lady was looking very sweetly at her host. Almost as if she was expecting her to do something. The old woman was wearing a purple hat on top of her long grey hair. The hat did not match her brown coat and bright red trousers. Her face was folded with many wrinkles but Fern could tell that she must have been very pretty as a young woman. She was still pretty now. Her eyes shone a deep green colour. A colour that Fern could not recall ever having seen before.

When Fern looked at her guest the lips of the old lady turned upwards into a smile. She had such a friendly, welcoming face. Fern was immediately at ease in the presence of this woman.

"I am sorry for the intrusion my dear but I can't stand up for as long as I used to. Now, I have been to five houses this morning looking for you Mrs. Calvern so I do hope that you can help me."

"I will do my best of course, Mrs….?"

"You can call me Heather. No need for formalities."

Fern was almost physical knocked by that name. Heather? She knew that it could not have been McGinley. Maybe it was just a coincidence.

"I believe you know something about that name, Fern. I

do also. You see, my father named me after his best friend. A young girl who killed herself in 1904. I take it that I do not need to inform you of the circumstances?

Fern shook her head. Could this be Jacob's daughter? If so she must be in her nineties by now if not more. She was unsure now about what was going to happen. Fern looked at this little old lady with suspicion. Why would Jacob's daughter be visiting her? How did she find out that she knew anything about Heather? Fern was still asking herself these questions as Heather continued to talk.

"I have read every one of your books. Very good, I must say. I know how it feels to have your life dictated to you by people who cannot understand you. I was married to a soldier after the war. I loved him, but he did not love me. He left me holding our baby a few years after the wedding. Life has been hard since but I loved my son and raised him to be better than his father. I must say, you certainly know how to write a story."

"Thank you, Heather."

It felt strange saying that name again. Fern had not uttered it for some time. Not since she had told her husband about her. Every time Fern had sat down to write another one of her books, she considered naming her protagonist Heather but she never did. She found it impossible to think about her for long. She was always thinking about her though, however briefly. Once, when she was reading a passage of her latest book, at a book signing, she realised how much that particular character reminded her of Heather. This made Fern uneasy. So much so that she made sure her next book was as far away from Heather's story as possible.

"I have something that I think you would be interested in. It is a diary. Not that of Heather McGinley, because I believe you know enough of that young girl already. No, this is a diary that my father wrote a few years before he married my mother. I do not know when exactly, he did not date the entries but I think it will be of interest to you."

The lady handed an old battered book to Fern. The pages were dog eared and turning brown but when Fern opened the pages she could see that the writing was clear enough to read. Heather raised herself cautiously from the chair and wandered towards the door.

"Read that. I will come back in a week. Then I will tell you why I really came to find you."

Fern looked at Heather, she was standing at the door of the living room and she was smiling at her.

"Make sure you get it finished. I'll show myself out."

Fern was too stunned by what had just happened to show good manners and Heather let herself out. She looked down at Jacob's diary. Did she really want to go through this again? It had been twenty years since she had read Heather's diary and she had still not been able to forget it. Would this new diary provide a deeper understanding of the events that occurred when Heather died? Or would it just reveal a whole different series of events? If that was the case Fern did not want to read the diary. She had spent years trying to get Heather's pain out of her mind. She did not want Jacob's pain as well. Even if it did help her to understand what had happened, what was she supposed to do about it? Then Heather's parting words came back to her.

"I will tell you why I really came to find you."

Why had she come? What possible use could Fern be to this woman? Fern sat and contemplated whether or not she should open the diary. She could still hear Andrew on the phone in the kitchen. He had no idea they had even had a visitor. Fern let out a long sigh. She knew full well that she would read the diary. In the end, her curiosity always got the better of her. That is how she had got involved in Heather's story in the first place. She gave in after just a few minutes with the thought that there was no point in delaying the inevitable.

Fern opened the diary at the first page and began to read.

Chapter Seven

Several years ago I lost a friend. She was just a child, as was I, and I loved her very much. More than I think I even knew. She killed herself and I have been stalked by her in my dreams since that dreadful day. I have been tormented with questions concerning her death and I have tried in vain to answer them. I have spent the last ten years of my life, through boyhood and into manhood, debating whether or not I could have saved her. I must slow down. I will start with why I am writing.

I have not kept a diary since I was a child, but I feel as if I cannot go on without putting my feelings down on paper. I am a grown man and my life thus far has been consumed with one girl. Heather McGinley. I knew her for just one year but even though I know that is true it seems like a knew her for a lifetime. We were both twelve when we met and thirteen when she died. I believe I was the only thing that kept her alive that long, if it weren't for our friendship I fear she would have gone sooner.

I have tried, but have been unable, to look at another woman with love and respect without seeing Heather's enchanting eyes and tremendous smile. I feel that I cannot lead a normal life without writing all that I feel. I must remove these painful memories from my mind lest I risk insanity.

She was my first love. I realise that now only in retrospect. At the time I saw only my best and only friend. She was beautiful but that did not matter to either of us at the age we were. Her long dark hair was kept tightly in a knot at the back of her head when she was at school but when we went out to play together, she would pull it out with great defiance and allow her untidy locks to spill over her shoulders.

I must have known she was beautiful but I never let such matters concern me. I never really saw her face when I looked at her. I only ever saw her, her mind, everything that was inside her. The only things I remember about her face were the eyes through which I could see her soul, and her remarkable smile. Every moment with her was a joy, even when she was telling me about the awful things that happened to her. Even when I feared I might lose her.

I met her for the first time one fateful afternoon, after we had both finished school for the day. We had both been punished by our teachers and were feeling hard done by, to say the least. When we saw each other we both had identical expressions of annoyance and frustration on our faces. We both found it funny when we recognised our own faces in each other's. We knew immediately that we understood each other. We were friends instantly and we walked home together discussing the awfulness of our teachers. How little they understood us and what horrors they unleashed upon us.

Her's went by the name of Sister Ruth. How I hate that woman. She punished Heather merely because she housed a creative mind and could not suppress it. Heather wrote relentlessly, she kept a diary and wrote poems and stories wherever there was space for her to do so. She even wrote on the walls of her bedroom when he parents took her paper away.

We relished those after school walks. We did not get to do as many as we had hoped because I was often detained by my teacher and Heather could not risk being too late coming home. The second day of our friendship was marred in this way. All I thought about was Heather and how disappointed she would be when she did not get the opportunity to vent her frustration over Sister Ruth. But when I saw her next she uttered no words of disapproval. She understood perfectly that I was unable to the prevent punishment. It was that day that I realised how special she was. It was so hard back then to find people who understood me. I know she felt the same way. I was always thinking about what my teacher was saying, but it was as if I was thinking beyond him at times. I felt as if I could have taught him more effectively than he taught me. When I allowed my frustrations to get the better of me, which is when I got into trouble. The problem of course was that I allowed that to happen too often.

I sought no salvation at home. My father, who had four sons before me, grew weary of my impertinence and took to lashing me whenever I was late home from school. It got to the point when he did not even wait for me to tell him I had been punished at school; he just presumed that I had been. This kind of injustice came to be expected in my life. My father was a figure of fear in my eyes. Whenever I saw him, I would audibly whimper at the threat that he posed. My mother was no help. She was too busy taking care of the needs of my father and brothers. I always came last at home. I was the last to be born so I always the last to be fed and bathed and cared for.

When my eldest brother got into trouble at school one day, my father took him into the study and spoke with him. I listened through the door, it was very clear that my eldest brother was the most important, he was told very sternly by my Father that he must behave and get a good education. He did not punish my brother but threatened him with a lashing if he got into trouble at school again. But it seems Father got bored of his children as they continued to come along and by the time I was getting into trouble he merely grumbled and punished me further. I was the youngest in the family and I could not wait to leave that Hell that I called home.

Heather was the only thing that kept me going in those days and I suppose she still does today. Her spirit is irrepressible and I see her in my dreams sometimes, smiling and laughing. At the weekends in the spring before she died I would tell my parents that I was going fishing at the river a mile from our home and would go and meet Heather. If they had known the truth, they would have prevented me from seeing her, and we could not allow that to happen. Heather's parents were made aware that she was enjoying the company of a young boy at the start of the year, and were highly suspicious of where she was going when she left the house. However, they were so pleased when Heather told them that she had a new female friend that they let her spend a great deal of time out of the house. Time that she chose to spend with me. I was thankful for this.

We would have the best times of our lives during those stolen hours. There was a piece of woodland not far from our schools, and we would go there from time to time to pick bluebells and climb trees. There was one tree that was our favourite. It was tall and strong and Heather told me that it reminded her of me, because it was tireless and could take whatever was thrown at it, and yet it remained.

This was a kind compliment and one that I try to live up to every day. When I think of the times in her life when she was happy, I can't understand why she took her life. Whenever we were alone together we had tremendous fun, even if we were in a boring place. How could someone with so much imagination not be able to see a different way out? The question, along with many others has haunted me for years. Could I have saved her? Could I have done something differently that would have kept her with me on this earth?

We climbed our tree until we were near the top. We knew that no one who walked below was able to see or hear us, so it became a secret hide out. One day a young couple were walking in the woods. They were strolling very thoughtfully and it was clear that they were courting. Heather found it very funny that a couple would steal away to the woods to be alone and she had an idea. She started making loud noises as if she were a ghost. The couple looked up towards us but failed to notice us, as the branches and leaves concealed us from their sight. I saw the fun that was to be had and I joined in with the noises. The couple were clearly disturbed by the increase in these frightening sounds and became agitated. It grew harder and harder to stifle the laughter, but we managed to keep the noise up long enough to scare the two people away. The man took his young lover by the arm and tried to drag her away from the haunted tree. It did seem to Heather and I as if the gentleman was rather more scared of the ghosts than his lady, who seemed rather more eager to stay.

We watched as the man grew more and more desperate until he cried at the lady to move away from the tree and leave the perilous woods with him. She did so reluctantly and it looked as if she was sneaking a smile at the new scarlet colour the gentleman had turned. Then we could stifle the laughter no more. We both started and did not stop for a good few minutes. It was so incredible to watch Heather laugh. Her smile was powerful enough to make even the saddest man glad. It grieves me to think that I was the only person who ever really saw it. Her head was thrown back with the laughter and her messy dark hair was thrown with it. Her eyes glistened and were alive. When I remember Heather, I try to think of her that day, laughing with the beauty of that great tree all around her.

Fern smiled at this. She thought back to Heather's ghost activity in her flat all those years ago. She had seen Heather's smile that day and felt her warmth and love. Fern knew that it wasn't Heather who was trying to hurt her in there. She put a hand to a scar on her face and put the diary down. She went into the kitchen and made a cup of tea. She drank it in there and thought about Jacob. She thought back to when Morgan had told her about Jacob's childhood diary. Why hadn't Jacob's daughter given Morgan the other diary, the one she was reading now? Maybe she had, but why would Morgan have wanted to conceal the rest of Jacob's life from her. Fern grew more and more desperate to find out more about Jacob. She put her empty mug on the side and went back into the living room. She picked up the diary and thought hard. She was getting dragged back again, deeper and deeper into a story that almost made her throw away her education twenty years ago. Fern hated herself for thinking sensibly, now was not the time to doubt herself. This could provide her with answers she wanted twenty years ago. She quickly persuaded herself that the only way to get over all of this pain was to finish it; to read all there was to read. She was in too deeply to turn back now.

Jacob's diary continued with no indication of date or time.

The worst thing that I think I ever did was lie to my friend. This lie has played on my mind for a great many years and I feel a great need to confess it. When we started the next school year I knew that Heather would have moved on from Sister Ruth's class and on to a more reasonable teacher. I had the same hope for myself. I had not warranted that the teacher who taught me in my second year at the school would be worse than the one from the first, but he was. My reputation had preceded me and my new teacher saw fit to punish me before I had even done anything wrong. However, he punished through humiliation so I was caned in front of all the others. I was very rarely detained. I endured his punishments, even long after Heather's death. It was hard at first, because I knew that such an amazing person had not been able to cope with a similar fate.

Over time I realised that if I could do anything now it was to survive. I believed that she could see me, that she was watching me. I did not want to disappoint her. Every time I saw my teacher stride towards me I thought about Heather for a moment. In that moment I could see her again. I could see how she would look if I allowed the punishment dealt out by the teacher to get the better of me. When I saw that look it made me forget the pain and humiliation. It made me strong. I thought of the oak tree and took whatever punishment I was given.

When I saw Heather after our first day of a new year, I decided to get in first and tell her how wonderful my new teacher was. I spent the entire walk home lying about my how wonderful he was and all because I thought Heather would have a similar tale to tell. You see, I did not think that she would want to be troubled by my difficulties when she had at last left her own behind. I believed that I was being noble. I intended to weather the storm of my second year at school like the tree in the woods that Heather had likened me to. I fear that this lie played a part in her undoing.

I learned too late, far too late, that Heather had been kept back in Sister Ruth's class for an extra year.

The day before I found out about Heather's misfortune at being kept back, I wrote in my diary what I had planned for the two of us after we leave school. I intended to go to London and study law. I wrote for hours how I would become the greatest prime minister that England had ever seen. I would abolish the school system immediately of course and come up with some way of teaching children without scaring them into obedience. The most important part of this plan was that I would send for Heather once I became the Prime Minister. We would live together and rule the country fairly and we would be happy.

She always wanted to be a writer so I would help her achieve that. It might seem like childish folly now but I would have done anything for her. If only she had asked me, I would have taken her away from her life before it got so much that she killed herself. Anything would have been better than that. We could have run away and begged on the streets until we had enough money to move on. We would have been happy because she would have been free. I would have been able to get a job somewhere and been able to support the two of us with no trouble. We would have been poor but that would not have mattered to her. All that mattered to Heather was being allowed to be herself. I believe that riches and comfort would have maybe prevented her from being her true self. They would have got in the way.

I wondered while I was writing in my diary back then if she would ever grow rich from her books and poems. I smiled slightly as I imagined her sitting beneath the great oak tree with her writing materials thinking up a wonderful tale to tell. I thought then about all the people who would read what she wrote there. The smiles that appeared in their faces as they read on and on through Heather's words. I thought about how one person loving a story she had written would be worth more to her than all the money in England. She would have been satisfied just sitting and writing for all eternity. But it was not to be.

I know now that I was the only person who was able to see what a wonderful person Heather truly was. She could have made such a difference to the world. It pains me now when I think of all the women who could have read Heather's books, stories and poems and been moved by them. She had such a fire inside of her that other women would have been moved by. Heather's fire will never go out as long as she is remembered. I wish that I could write of her properly. I would tell her story but I fear that I would not do her justice. I am sure that I will find someone who can tell this story one day.

The writing seemed to stop there. The next entry was in a darker ink so Fern took this opportunity to take a break. She had been happy when she heard of Jacob's new teacher from Morgan. The information that it was all a lie hurt. She did not want to know what else there was hiding in these pages. What other secrets would be revealed? Fern almost felt Jacob's pain growing as she read his diary. Her heart was flooding with emotion. So much so that she felt that soon she would be unable to breathe. She did not want to know; she put down the diary and stood up. She couldn't believe it, after all these years! She felt like she wanted to cry but couldn't. Her face was screwed up with sorrow but no tears came. Frustrated, Fern slumped back onto the sofa. Why did she have to do this? Why did Jacob's daughter have to give her his diary? The pain inside her would only grow. It would not subside. Fern knew this but she knew she would read on, she had to; she opened the diary and forced herself to read.

When I cast my eyes skyward I see clouds drifting across the sky. It reminds me of the day when Heather and I were at the well and we lay on our backs watching the clouds go by. We would argue about what they looked like. There was one cloud that was clearly a horse but Heather was insistent that it was in the shape of a rabbit. I see clouds sometimes in the shapes of rabbits. I believe that Heather has sent them to tease me. I smile when I see those clouds.

When I stood over Heather's grave at her funeral I realised for the first time that she was truly gone. There was no way around the fact now. She was in the ground and she was not going to come back. She was dead. I did not allow myself to believe it up until then. I regretted so much about the last year as I looked at the words carved into the rock of her tombstone. Why had I lied? Why did I not tell her there was hope? I asked myself for the first time that day if I had killed her, and I have asked myself that same question every day since. She has haunted my every step and my every word. When I sleep, I dream of her. When I see beautiful women, I see Heather. When I look into the eyes of some one I care about, I see the shining blue eyes of Heather staring back at me. She is in the air that I breathe, the food that I eat, the water that I drink. She is all around me and inside me. My love for Heather will never die. My regret at allowing her to slip away from me will only ever grow and grow. I promised her that I would always be with her.

That day when we watched the clouds pass over our heads I said to her that I would never leave her. I said that if she ever wanted to leave that she must come and fetch me and I would go with her. I told her that if she wanted to get away, if she wanted to escape that I would go with her. All she had to do was ask and I would have done anything for her. So why didn't she?

Why didn't she ask me to die alongside her? I would have done it, I would have jumped into that well with her, and I would have fetched the rope and the rock. I would have tied the rope around our waists and I would have jumped with her. Why did she do it alone? Why did she leave me all alone? I loved her and she left me. I loved her so much and I should have told her. Why did I lie to her? Why did I make her feel like she was the only one who was unhappy? I would have taken my life alongside her. I would have died for her. But instead she did it alone. I let her die alone and for that I can never forgive myself. Now I must live with this. When I die, I pray that I will see Heather again and she will smile and her eyes will shine brighter than ever and she will tell me off, she will tell me how foolish I have been and she will dry my tears. She would not abandon me as I did her. She would never allow me to face anything that was scary or painful alone. She would have stood beside me, held my hand. She would have helped me do whatever I had to do to be happy. I failed her. I let her down. How could I have let her down? I ask myself every day what I could have done to save her. Maybe it could have been just one word, or one smile that saved her. What if she was looking for something from me, some sign of hope or understanding? Why could I have not seen it? Why couldn't I have shown her that I did understand?

I fear though, more than anything, that when I die Heather will not be there. Part of me believes she will not be there because I do not deserve to see her again. I let her down in life so why would she want to help me in death? So I will live my life and I will pass the amazing story of Heather on to my daughter. I will ensure that I pass this story on and she will live forever in their hearts.

Fern felt tears come streaming down her face as she read this. She had not cried for Heather in such a long time and she felt the familiar ache come back to her. Fern had not realised how much Jacob had loved Heather. The tragedy of Heather McGinley worsened in Fern's mind and she felt for Jacob's severe loss. The flood of emotion was still welling but Fern no longer feared it consuming her, she had to know how this story ended. She continued to read.

I lost part of myself that day. There is a hole, an empty space inside me that I fear will never be filled, unless by some miracle. I cried while at Heather's graveside. I felt the tears come and was unable to stop. There were clouds in the sky that day but they moved as my tears ran and the sun came out, drying my face. I looked up and was sure that I saw a cloud the shape of my dear friend's face, albeit it very briefly. The cloud disappeared and I was all alone.

The clouds gathered again as I walked home and as I fell asleep that night listening to vicious rolls of thunder. I woke up the next day with a heavy heart and the memory of dark dreams. With no hope within me that I would ever find a way to ease the pain of Heather's passing, I wandered into the woods. Images of Heather and myself playing there flashed briefly before my eyes and before I knew it I was at our tree. But something was wrong. There was a massive branch lying before me, stopping me from taking my usual route to the tree. Then I realised. I looked up and I could see right up to the sky, when previously the great tree had prevented it. The branch on the floor had been severed from the tree in the storm.

It was not what I wanted to see. I looked up and saw a great scar where the branch had been. I named it Heather's scar and left. I felt my pain pour into that ugly scar. My heart was slightly gladdened that the loss of Heather had left a wound as great as mine on another living thing. I believed then, and still do now that the tree that reminded Heather of me, had given in against the storm because its grief of losing a friend was so great.

Fern laid down the diary and wept. All the loss suffered by this one man was unbearable. He really had loved Heather. Fern had felt the loss before, back in her old flat, but this was immeasurable. She was now feeling the pain from the one person Heather had cared about. She was feeling it first hand and it hurt her. It felt as if someone had stabbed Fern in the chest. Fern went over to the drinks cabinet and poured herself a glass of whiskey. The shock of the alcohol pulled her back to her senses and she read on.

I feel like I have relieved a great pain from my heart. Heather was so special and it was a truly great tragedy that she was taken from the world before she had a chance to leave her mark and make a difference.

My pain will never wholly leave me and I fear that a dull ache will live in my heart for eternity. I know that I will see her again, when I die. I must have faith in this belief. I do not wish to see her again until I am ready. There is much I must do. This journal was one of those things and I am glad to write that it has fulfilled its purpose. I am less grieved than I was at the commencement of these pages. I must now look to the future. I will close this book and I must never reopen it. If I do I fear I will only reopen the wounds these words have finally closed. I will keep the book however. I will keep it and pass it on to my daughter. I feel as if I owe Heather the chance of living forever in memory. For now, that is the only way she will live forever. When she was alive, she had the chance to grow and become a writer. Now it is up to those that are living to find means to help her be remembered. She deserves to be remembered. She touched my life in such a way; I believe she can touch others. It is a great injustice and an even greater tragedy that she was taken from this earth so young. It would be a disaster if she was taken from the memory of those who live

Fern smiled as she realised that she was reading the diary with Jacob's consent. Jacob was a man that Fern had grown to respect greatly and she was pleased that she was helping to accomplish his goal on writing this diary in the first place. She was sure that she knew it already. She was a writer after all. She had the means to complete a dream that had existed for over a hundred years.

Chapter Eight

There was a knock on the door. It had been exactly a week, to the hour since Jacob's daughter Heather had given Fern the diary that changed everything. During that week Fern had spent many hours in her study, looking over the brief account of the life of Heather McGinley she had written twenty years ago again and again. Her husband left her alone, still thinking that she was writing her children's story. Still unaware that it was Heather who had inspired that idea in the first place.

Fern buried herself in the months of discovery that had taken place years previously. She forced herself to remember everything. Even the things she would rather have forgotten. No tears came to Fern during this reminiscence. She was filled with a sense of duty. She knew that Jacob had lived only because of his eagerness to remember Heather, and Fern knew she had a role to play in that purpose. Fern also knew that that role would be given to her by Jacob's daughter when she returned to Fern's house. Fern had read the diary in a day, it was not very long but she had read every word carefully in order to not misunderstand a word of it. The remaining six days of the time that Heather had given Fern ticked by slowly.

Fern busied herself with whatever she could. She was stuck somewhere between wanting to forget about everything and being desperate to recall every detail of Heather's life. It was torturous. Fern could not relieve her discomfort because she had no one to confide in. Andrew cared deeply for his wife but he would not understand. He had a tendency to rationalise everything. If Fern had one weakness that she was unashamed of, it was that she had to keep the magic in her life. If she spoke to Andrew he would take it away. He would make her feel as if the diary was nothing new and the new Heather was just a desperate and sad old woman.

Fern did not want that. She needed this diary to be special. Somewhere inside her she knew it was. Her fear of feeling that same pain that she had felt for Heather was the only thing that made her doubt if she would want to see Jacob's daughter again. She even allowed the thought of not letting Heather back into her home cross her mind. But she soon banished these thoughts from her mind. She had come through scarier things than this before.

When the week had spent itself Fern waited for Heather to turn up, her fears allayed, and when she did Fern's rush to the door surprised her husband. But he was more than used to his wife's unusual moods when she was working on a new book. He decided to take himself upstairs. Fern opened the door and saw Heather standing in the rain with a look of determination in her eyes. All Fern's fear returned. She knew what Heather was about to say was going to change something. She just wished she knew what that something was.

Heather walked in to the hallway without an invitation, she did not need one. She knew that Fern would not refuse her entry after what she had just read.

"I do not need to ask if you have read what I gave you because I know that you have. I can see it in your eyes. My father gave that diary to me when I was twenty. That is when he died. The doctors say that it was a form of cancer but I know that he had given up on life. My mother always knew where my father's love was. He did love her, but his love for my mother was nothing in comparison to the love he bore for Heather. But my mother was a loyal woman and she cared deeply for all of us. I had four brothers, all born before me. But my father wanted a daughter. I think that in his heart he wanted to make a young girl's life a joy. He wanted to do that for Heather. I don't really know when I was told about my namesake. All I know is that I don't remember ever not knowing. I always knew that I was named after her and I often asked my father to tell me the story of Heather

McGinley before I went to bed.

"He would tell me how the beauty of the world was visible in her eyes. He could not look into them without smiling. He would cherish every moment he spent with her. He told me one night before I went to sleep that when he thought about Heather he could see everything in a bright white light. When she died, that light went out and he found it hard to see anything at all. When he described his grief to me I would cry. He said he felt a heavy weight in his stomach, a weight that was lifted a little when I was born. He told me that if I achieved nothing else in my life, I had helped a man to smile again. I loved my father very much. It makes me sad that he was such a restless spirit. He only had one aim in life. I am here, Fern, to achieve that aim for my father.

"I need your help. You can write a story beautifully. I can't. Even if I could I don't think that I have enough time and energy to complete an entire book. What I am asking of you is that you write a book for me. It was clear from my father's writings that he wanted to immortalise his friend in the form she loved so much. That is what he wanted. You are the only person who can do it.

"You can write so beautifully and you understand her. You have met her as well, after a fashion. I know that you must get requests all the time for this kind of thing, but I assure you that I have a greater reason than any woman can give you. I have always loved reading books that women have written. But there are many stories that have never been told. Stories of women who were never able to write. Women who were so trapped by the society that they lived in that they could never get their stories heard. But we both know a story. We have both been told of a great writer who never lived to see her story told. But we can tell it Fern. We can tell the world the story of Heather McGinley. Will you help me?"

Fern sat for some time without knowing what to say. She

had thought about Heather during the writing of every one of her books but had never intended to write a book about her. Fern had experienced something life changing in that flat. She had witnessed a story in her dreams and on paper. A story written for her. Readymade characters and so much emotion. But there was still doubt nagging at Fern. She did not feel as if she could write this story yet.

The old lady did not take her eyes off Fern. She was waiting with a patience she had learned in her many years. She wanted so badly for Fern to say yes to her proposal, but she knew that she could not rush things. Fern's face bore a look of confusion. Heather could see that Fern was concerned about publishing the story. She thought that she could probably persuade Fern if she wanted, but the last thing that Heather wanted was to get Fern on side if she wasn't all the way behind the idea. She gazed at Fern, willing her to say, 'Yes, of course I will do it.'

"I know that Heather's story is an important one." Fern said after great contemplation. "I understand that there are many people in this world who would love to hear her story, people who would be inspired by it the way that I have been. The way you have been. But I don't know if I am able to share my experience with people. It was deeply personal and it changed my whole life. I don't know if I can help you."

"You don't see do you? You have written nine books. Nine! Every page of every one of your books is about Heather. I can see it. I can see her in your words and your stories. You write of young girls with a desire to become writers. When I read about them having obstacles put in their way, I see Heather. I see Heather when you describe the hopelessness people feel when their dreams are dashed. And most importantly, I see Heather when I look at you. She is deep inside your eyes. She lives inside you and she writes her stories through you. You look at me with the pain I always felt when I thought about her. You have something inside you that is screaming to get out. You need to let it breathe. Heather is inside you in the same way that she is inside me. I have shared the story with no one. I too know how it feels to have it inside you. It is painful but beautiful at the same time. Heather's spirit was too strong not to have endured all this time. We are the last people on this earth who can tell the story Fern. Will you immortalize her for the world?"

With this, Heather stood and walked towards the door. She had left her father's diary on Fern's coffee table. She did not need it anymore. She had given it to the one person in the entire world who could help her, who could do what her father had always wished he could do.

Fern sat as the old lady left the house. She sat and thought about Heather. The same way that she had done all those years ago when she had heard the whole story in her flat. Fern was confused once more. There was so much emotion running through her mind. She wanted to help Heather and tell the story but she didn't feel as if she could. Her head was pounding. She could feel her pulse beating hard at her temples. It would be so easy to do it. She could just reach down and pick up the pen in front of her and write. She could write until her fingers were bleeding. So why didn't she? What was stopping her? She did not understand. She wanted to tell this story. She realised now that she always had. She was annoyed with herself now.   Heather McGinley had died because she couldn't write. She never even had the chance to ponder over whether she should write a book or not. Fern picked up the pen but she could not write. She just stared at the paper. Her hands were shaking so much now that the pen dropped back onto the table. Why couldn't she do it? She sat back in her chair and stared at Jacob's diary. This was when she noticed something else that Heather had left behind.

It was a small card. It was lying on the coffee table. Fern picked it up and looked at it. Written upon it was the name Longwood Mental Asylum. Fern stared at this piece of paper. Where had she heard of Longwood Mental Asylum before? Then it came to her. Every drop of blood in her body ran cold. Longwood Mental Asylum. That was where Sister Ruth had been committed. A wave of understanding came over Fern. She realised so many things at once that she was unable to think straight for a number of minutes. She had the address for the institute where Sister Ruth spent her life after Heather had killed herself. She could find this place. She could find out more about Sister Ruth. That was what had been stopping her. She knew about Jacob. She knew about Heather. She knew very little of Sister Ruth. The only time she had seen her was in her dreams. That evil face had stared at her as if she was lower than dirt. Fern's excitement made way for anger. Fern was going to go to Longwood Mental Asylum. She was going to find out exactly what was going on in that diabolical woman's head.

The anticipation of gaining that knowledge allowed for excitement to swell once more inside Fern. She realised she was still sitting down staring at the card in her hand. She had to get up. Fern rose from her chair and put her coat and shoes on with only thoughts of Sister Ruth running through her mind.

Fern searched for her car keys. What new insights would this asylum have to offer Fern? Would she get to see what was going on in Sister Ruth's head? Would she get to see the story from Ruth's side? This last question stuck and Fern stopped still. She had not thought about Sister Ruth's side of the story. What would she discover? What if Heather had been an insufferable student? The last thing that Fern wanted was to start sympathising with Sister Ruth. Fern stood for a moment.

There were no real thoughts going through her mind. She did not even hear her husband ask if she wanted a cup of tea. She simply stood. Fear again flooded her mind. For the last twenty years of her life she had believed that Heather was an innocent party. What would she do if she discovered that wasn't the case? After a time Fern grew determined. She knew that Heather had not been punished through necessity. No child could have possibly deserved that. Fern picked up the car keys that had been on the table next to where her coat had been hanging and left the house.

Driving to the asylum was difficult. The address was clear and Fern knew where she was supposed to go but if the address was accurate then the asylum itself must have been well off the beaten track. Fern thought about the practicalities of building a mental asylum and supposed that if it was built in the middle of nowhere then ordinary people wouldn't notice it. Out of sight, out of mind.

Fern considered the location a little more. The thought of wide open green spaces and trees that went on as far as you could see had somewhat of a calming effect on her. Maybe that was the reason, she pondered. Calming a distressed mind by taking it away from the busy streets and putting it in a natural environment seemed like a sensible idea.

The town roads that weaved around the area where Fern lived soon turned into country lanes. Fern drove quickly. The road she was on suddenly turned into a twisty single track but Fern was too deep in thought to notice. A loud blast from a car she barely missed caused her to slam on her brakes and realise where she was. The other driver had also stopped.

"What the bloody Hell do you think you are doing?"

"I'm sorry, I er, I didn't realise."

"You didn't realise what? That there was a huge red car driving towards you? It's not exactly difficult to see that this road is narrow, love."

"I know, I'm sorry. Look, I don't suppose you know where I can find Longwood Mental Asylum do you?"

"Why, are you in need of urgent treatment? No, I don't know where it is and if you don't mind I'm in a bit of a hurry…"

Fern saw where he was gesticulating and reversed her car into the entrance to a field. She did not appreciate the man's sarcasm. She drove on slowly and looked out for the asylum. She was sure it must be close by.

Fern turned down a foreboding road and drove uncomfortably down it for about five minutes. She stopped the car when she saw it. A tall thin gothic building protruding unnaturally out of the ground. It belonged in a horror movie and Fern sensed that what had happened inside this fortress belonged in one as well.

The gates were made of iron and a modern lock on the handles looked out of place. Fern could not get in. She looked around for some way to summon help when her eyes fell on an ancient looking bell. To say that it was weathered would be insufficient. Fern doubted that the bell would hold together if she tried to ring it, let alone make a sound but she thought she had better try anyway. She walked over to it, reached inside and rang. There was a dull thud but the bell stayed in one piece so Fern was at least relieved about one thing.

She began to worry if anyone had heard her though. What was she going to do if she couldn't get in? The thought that she was all alone and no one knew where she was, was beginning to scare her. There came the sound of a car behind her. Fern turned and saw a confused looking man driving a classic jaguar towards the gates where Fern was standing. He got out of his car revealing a large frame and great height. Fern looked back at the car and wondered how he had managed to fit inside. His booming voice asked a question that demanded an answer.

"Can I help you?

"Hi, yes, sorry. I am looking for Longwood Asylum."
The man laughed a kind laugh.

"I'm not sure what you've been told but this building hasn't been a hospital in quite some time. This is my home, along with several others. It was converted into flats a long time ago."

Fern stepped back. The disappointment she felt clearly showed on her face.

"If you are looking for a mental health facility the hospital in the city has a dedicated wing. I can find the address if you like."

His concern for her was genuine she felt, perhaps he thought she needed help for herself.

"No, thank you though. I know where it is."

Fern smiled at the man who was still frowning with concern, and walked back to her car.

Fern knew where the hospital was. They were places you inevitably became more familiar with as you aged. She drove deep in thought. Why had Heather left her that note if the asylum wasn't there anymore? She did look very old, maybe her memory was failing.

After spending half an hour looking for a parking space Fern managed to get herself into the hubbub of the hospital reception area. She would have preferred to have still been in the nice countryside setting of the old asylum. How did anyone ever recover in all this chaos?

The receptionist was very calm all things considered but when Fern asked her what she wanted her face turned from sunny to gloomy.

"I'm writing a book about a girl who took her own life in 1904. Her teacher went insane afterward and was committed to Longwood Mental Asylum I wonder do you know any files or records from that hospital?"

The receptionist's name badge read 'Cassie' and she listened carefully to what Fern was staying, then shifted in her seat as she answered.

"We do have historical records from the asylum but we will have to get someone to fetch them. And it might take some time to get that organised. Take a seat and I will see what I can do for you."

Fern sat and waited. The receptionist had given no

indication of how long this might take but Fern wasn't expecting a quick turnaround. Over the course of the next few hours she was approached and spoken to by several members of the hospital's administration team and eventually she was lead into a small, windowless room. She would get to see Ruth's files but she would have to read them here in this room and not take them off hospital property.

Fern agreed and commenced waiting again, but in a different room this time.

The door swung open and a fresh faced young woman with a genuine smile walked in.

"You're Fern Calvern aren't you? My wife loves your stories."

"Thank you." Fern mumbled, she had forgotten for a moment that she was no longer a 20 year old student finding out about all this for the first time.

"Here you are, I will have to leave this with you to go through. I just look after the files, I don't know what's in them. Any problems, just give me a shout. I'll be on the desk just down the corridor on the right."

Fern thanked the woman and stared down at the pile of papers on the desk. Unsure what she would find. Nervous of opening this can of worms again, but desperate to find out more.

The first thing that her eyes fell on was a photograph. It was very old and grainy with its sepia colouring giving away its age.

Fern squinted at the photo of Sister Ruth. She looked exactly the same as she had done in Fern's final dream. Right before Ruth's spirit had attacked Fern. She was an ugly woman. Her face was screwed up and her lips turned down in a permanent frown. Fern could see her rosary hanging around her neck. This sight sickened her. This woman claimed to be doing the work of God and in doing so, killed a girl. The irony was not worth thinking about.

Fern opened the folder up and saw the sheets of paper inside. There were so many. They looked to be dated and kept in order. That would make it easier for her. She would start at the beginning. Although, she doubted she would be able to read through all of them in the short time she had. Fern recalled how she had skipped the pages of Heather's diary and hoped that ghostly interference would not play a part in this isolated room. Outside she could hear the muted sounds of a busy hospital. The clunking of gurney wheels and the chatter of nurses.

Fern picked up a folder marked, 'Patient #1075 B, Sister Ruth Ambridge. Dated 12/10/1905.' A year after the death of Heather. She opened the folder cautiously. It was as if she was opening a door to a different world. She was about to find out what Sister Ruth really thought about Heather McGinley. When she began to read she discovered that most of the papers were letters Ruth had written whilst in the asylum. The first paper was different. It looked like a checking in report from when Ruth was admitted.

Patient #1075 B. She is a female of around five feet and four inches tall. She is slight in build and there are signs of recent and severe weight loss. She is between the ages of forty and fifty. We have been unable to find the record of her birth and the patient is unwilling to divulge her age to us so this is an estimate. She has brown hair which is quite long and unkempt. She will not allow us to cut it or comb it so it remains untidy. She is a woman of faith having spent her entire working life as a nun in a Catholic school for girls by the name of Saint Agnes's. The patient has been sent to us following the death of one of the school's pupils. The pupil in question died as the result of an accident but it became apparent soon after her death that the Sister had a great dislike for the patient and upon learning this, the patient has grown confused as to whether the girl died because of the afore mentioned hatred.

Fern sat back and felt the anger she had known for twenty years rise again in her heart. She had forgotten that Heather's death had been labelled as an accident. But Sister Ruth knew. She had read the diary. She must have known that Heather killed herself that day. Fern continued to read, moving onto the first of the letters. It wasn't clear who they were but it was written in the hand of Sister Ruth.

I have prayed for weeks and months and God has answered my prayers by bringing me here to this forsaken place. He does indeed work in mysterious ways. I am spoken to like a child and ushered about to do my work. I clean the walls and the floors and the toilets and the sinks. I do not mind, cleanliness is next to Godliness and it does well to live in a clean place.

There are many other women here. Some are sinful women who had a child without a husband. Some have given in to the evils of drink. Others are merely imbeciles. I have asked the nurses if I could perhaps be permitted to teach the other patients. Maybe put some values into their lives. I am not sure if it will work with those women though. Many are too busy crying.

Fern put down the paper. There was more to the letter but she had to take a break. Reading Ruth's words and seeing her hatred for people seep out of the page was too much. Another letter caught Fern's eye and she picked it up.

She was such a foolish girl. She was always running around with silly little ideas in her head. Ideas above her station. She actually believed that she could have become a writer. She could not have achieved any such feat. She was unable even to learn simple Latin phrases. I find it ironic though that her desire to be a writer is what got me into this predicament in the first place. This young girl did a mischievous thing, and she kept a diary. In this diary there were pages and pages of evil words about me and the things that I did to her. It was upon reading this diary that I began to think. I asked myself, could I have led this poor innocent girl to her death? I rubbished this idea immediately of course, this particular girl was not innocent at all, and I cannot see that I, a servant of our Lord God, could be capable of forcing upon a person the act of a mortal sin.

The whole thing was preposterous. She had caused me so much grief when she was alive and now that she was dead she is still the source of all my woes. I think that goes to show just how much of a naughty little girl she was. Always thinking of different ways in which to pain me and make my life a waking nightmare.

I know that she was not unintelligent. I knew that she could answer the questions I gave her and solve the problems that I set but she simply refused to cooperate. Noxious child! She died the way she should have. She died by being foolish. I tried in vain you see to make her a lady. Her family's position was precarious, she needed to marry well for their sake. Her father was a mere bank clerk and she had no brothers to help. The only hope for her to have a fruitful life, outside of the church of course was to marry well. Her parents had chosen a delightful boy. He was a few years older than her but his father was the bank manager and the boy was lined up to take the same path when he was old enough.

It would not have been a great improvement on

her childhood wealth but it would have been comfortable. But she was stubborn and ambitious. Two qualities I am afraid are not welcome in little girls. No man wants to take a wife who will put herself first before him. I put it upon myself to train her right. I cared about the girls in my care, I really did. But there is little I can do when they do not care about themselves.

The thing about Heather that was the most disturbing I thought was the friendship that she had with a little boy who attended the boy's public school near to Saint Agnes's. His name was Jacob. He was the one I believe responsible for the death of that poor girl.

He was very similar to Heather. He was very ill-behaved and was ill-treated too. But he deserved his punishments. As did his little friend. I learnt from the diary she left behind that she met up with Jacob frequently to discuss how much they both hated me. I was not at all shocked by this piece of information. I would have thought it odd indeed if a girl I was forced to punish as much as Heather did not protest when out of my ear range. In fact, I found these comments about me most satisfactory. It meant of course that my punishments were working.

That young man should have made Heather aware that she was mistaken in her ambitions. He ought to have told her that she could dream all she liked about becoming a writer, or a traveller, or any other strange life she may have planned for herself. The fact of the matter is that she was a girl who would have grown into a woman. This means that all ambitions are to be drowned at once. She had no business to look any further than a life as a dutiful wife. She was blinded by her ambition and her sinful pride. She could not see that the only path she could take was the same one that her mother trod. She was forced into a corner. A situation that could yield nought but sin.

Yes, I do believe that Heather took her own life. I believe that she was foolish enough to do it. I think it goes to show what ambition does to little girls. It drives them to insanity. And it was entirely that young man Jacob's fault. If he had not filled her with false dreams and silly ambitions, she would never have been driven into a place where she felt so trapped.

Yes, I know that Heather blamed me for her demise and I do not hold that against her. What I need to say is that she was unable to see that it was Jacob, telling her what she wanted to hear. Telling her that she could become whatever she wanted to be that drove her to take her own life. I had nothing to do with it. I was trying to help her. I was trying to save her. But she was not willing to be saved. She listened to Jacob and she was led to sin. He killed her and what is worse is that he did it without taking the blame.

Fern could not believe what she was reading. Did Sister Ruth really suppose that it was Jacob who had been responsible for Heather's death? Fern recoiled from this thought. It was impossible that he had driven her to take her own life. Wasn't it? Surely you cannot punish someone for helping a young girl realise a dream. Sister Ruth had been blamed by Heather herself for her death and Ruth had not even considered that it could be her fault. Jacob had not been blamed by anyone except himself. Fern thought that this fact alone proved that Jacob had not been to blame. He had obviously cared about Heather so much that he sought ways he could have stopped her. Ruth on the other hand had sought ways to clear her name.

Fern was incensed. She had hated Sister Ruth before but

her hatred was growing with every new word that she read. How could this woman be so deluded? It was so clear to everyone else. Her, Heather, Jacob, Morgan, Jacob's daughter. Why was Ruth the only one involved who couldn't see her guilt? Fern continued to read the letters.

The problem I had with this Heather girl was that the path she was supposed to take was littered with an imagination. Everywhere she looked there were ideas and thoughts that were indecent in a young girl. The Lord did not smile on that girl. He made her life hard. That is what God does. He tests us.

She was an ungrateful child and so God gave her a challenge. He tempted her with ambition and pride. When she failed to turn from these emotions and embrace Him instead He punished her. He sent her to me and I was made to punish her. That is where I came into His plan for Heather. She was a sinner and God gave me permission to punish her on this earth before she was finally sent to Hell. That is where she is now of course. She committed a mortal sin, she destroyed God's gift of life. She went to Hell with all the other sinners. That is where she belongs. I would like to see her write her little poems in there with the red hot whip of the devil on her back. She wrote in that diary that she would rather be in Hell if she knew that I would be in Heaven. I suppose then that she got her wish. She is in Hell and I will go to Heaven when the Lord sees fit to take me to his side. I cannot help but wonder if she is regretting what she said now.

I have always maintained that one must not ask God for anything. He will give you what you deserve when you have earned it. She asked Him for too much and without even doing anything in return. They say that the Lord works in mysterious ways. But in Heather's case, I think it is easy enough to see what he was doing.

I have always been a deeply religious woman. Ever faithful to the Catholic Church. My father was an Irishman who moved over to England to find work. He was never a man of the cloth but he did follow the religion strictly. My mother was English, she was converted to Catholicism by my father. They had twelve children in total. I was number seven. I do not know what became of my brothers and sisters. I became a nun when I was fourteen and never heard from any of them again. I was glad of this however; there were rebels in the family. I know for a fact that one of my brothers did not adhere to the rules of the church. He must be dead by now judging by the way he lived while I was still at home. Stumbling home drunk and smelling of women. He is no doubt keeping that McGinley girl company.

I went into teaching willingly but it was not as fulfilling as I had imagined. Some of the children I taught were beyond my help. None so much as Heather of course. Although some did come exceptionally close. I will not bore you with their stories. I am sure you are eager to discover why it is that I am here. You have heard me talk many times and I am in no doubt that you find me most normal. No, the reason I am here is because I did my job and there was one person, one girl who decided that it wasn't good enough. She thought too much and she developed ideas that were not accurate. She believed that I was evil. I ask you , how can I be evil when I am here to do the work of God? Every action I took against that girl was in the name of the Lord.

No, the problem with that girl was her imagination. She allowed it to take over her mind. And when it did she believed that she was above my teachings. She never was able to understand that I was right. I was always right. That is what made my job at Saint Agnes's so hard. I would tell my students the truth and I would teach them what they needed to know. However, you do come across one every once in a while who sees things differently. The Devil takes these girls. Girls like Heather and girls like the ones who fraternised with my brother. And I am glad that he does. I do not wish to spend another moment in the company of Heather McGinley.

I do not like it when I fall asleep. It is true that I ask the nurses ever so nicely if they will give me something to stop the dreams but instead they give me things to make me fall asleep. And when I do, I fear for my sanity. She comes to me in my dreams, Heather. The Devil sends her back to me as I sleep to allow her to cause some final mischief. No amount of prayer helps me to stop these dreadful visions. She talks to me. She tells me that it is my fault that she is dead. I know it is not. It cannot be my fault because I am a nun. Nuns are not responsible for ruining lives they are there to help people. I do not understand how anyone can believe a holy woman capable of murder.

I never strayed from the teachings of the Lord. I never went to bed with a man, I have maintained a sober life, and I have never missed a session of prayer. I am a good woman. I have read the bible every day of my life and I know it well. I have taken in every word and I have followed what it has taught me. It is in the Ten Commandments that 'thou shalt not kill'. If I have followed the word of the Lord so strictly my entire life, how can I be responsible for the death of a young girl? No, she killed herself. She took her life and as she did so she committed a sin.

She is in Hell and it is all her doing. If she had

followed the bible like I told her time and time again she would not have died. Satan would not have tempted her with cowardice. She died because she sinned, not me. I find it disgraceful that a twelve year old can accuse a nun of sin. I doubt that she had even ever picked up a bible outside of my lessons. She had no faith and so she was doomed. I even caught her once defiling the word of God by writing her unholy words in the bible. I was so enraged I caned her there in front of the whole class. And as I did so I felt the wrath of God flow through me. I felt righteous.

She still tells me though. Every night she tells me that I am evil, that I killed her. She tells me that she is in Heaven where the Lord God greeted her and told her that she was safe. She tells me that I will never see her there because I am destined to wander the barren deserts of Hell for all eternity. She shows me things too. She shows me how she died and how much pain she was in. But the pain she suffers is not the pain of death; it is the pain that drove her to death. She shows me Hell in these dreams. She tells me she is taking me to see where I will go when I die. I see a house. I believe that it is Heather's house. We are both inside and she is showing me her pain in there. She shows me writing on the walls and while we are there she tells me she will show me what is next. I see nothing. There is nothingness stretched far all around me. I cannot see but I can feel. I am hot, too hot. I can find no relief because I am already naked. I look but there is no relief. I still cannot see but I can hear now. I can hear a soft noise like that of a bumble bee in summer. It is inside my head and it will not cease. It grows louder and louder as I try to think where I am or how I got there. I take a step forward to try and escape but I do not move forward, I begin to fall. I can feel air rushing past me, but it is not cool, it does not sooth me. It burns instead. When I land, I am in water. Again, it is not cool. I cannot swim. The sound in my head grows louder.

Then I wake. Sometimes, I wake up and I believe the words she whispers in my ear as I sleep. She can be so convincing. I feel as if now more than ever I need to show God that I love him. He needs me to continue his divine teachings. That is why I try to teach the people in here the way of the Lord, but they will not listen to me. They are already doomed. They just look at me and sometimes they laugh. Can you believe that? They laugh as I describe what Hell is like. I try with infinite patience to make them see how they can improve, how they can please the Lord but they do not care to hear it. They would rather continue with their sins. They say things about God having forsaken them and perhaps they are right, perhaps they are too far gone. But I dedicated my life to serving the Lord and I must persevere.

Heather was such a pretty little thing. It is such a shame that she chose to walk the path of that leads to damnation. She could have married well and had a happy life with many children to make her complete. She could have made me happy. I would have heard about her life and been pleased that I had taught her. But no. She had to insist on defying me. Well, I will not allow the people here to do the same. I will go to any lengths I have to so they will at least learn the errors of their ways even if they are beyond any hope of salvation. I will make them listen, Doctor. Those who laugh and turn away will soon be begging for me to teach them more of God's divine words.

Fern was finding it hard to believe the words that were coming out of Sister Ruth's mouth. She was actually defending herself. It irritated Fern that a woman can be so proud that she cannot even admit that she made mistakes, that she was wrong about something. Even worse than this, she could not work out why Ruth had not learned from these mistakes. She was still trying to teach people the way that she taught Heather. She still believed that she had done nothing wrong.

Fern put down this report and glanced around the papers in front of her. She wanted to know more about why Ruth had treated Heather that way. Fern found another letter that caught her attention. It started with the words she had been longing to see.

People ask me about my reasons She was a very badly behaved girl and she needed discipline. Oh, very well. There is more to it than all that of course. Heather may have been naughty beyond repair, but she was also very intelligent. She had noticed that she was the only member of my class who was punished so severely. There are a number of reasons for this. First of all, when Heather first came to the school it was clear to me that she would be trouble. She would fidget terribly.

My eyes were constantly distracted by her movements and it made it very hard for me to concentrate. Any girl who causes instant disruption like this will not fare well in my class. I decided to take her in hand from the start. This proved useless. After a time, I believe she may even have been immune to its lashes. She would scream in pain of course but she soon sounded less distressed. She may have even been enjoying it. Maybe she saw the cane as a sign that she had succeeded in infuriating me. After a week or two of teaching her, I began to correspond with the girl's parents. The McGinley's were very nice people, they always are. But they had a problem. It seems that Heather had tried to inform them that I was punishing her without reason. I assure you now, there was always a reason to punish Heather McGinley.

However, her mother in particular was very concerned and she wrote to me so that I could reassure her I was doing the best I could to set her daughter straight. I did of course explain myself completely and I am pleased now to say that Mrs. McGinley understood at once. The information we then exchanged in our letters was quite different. She informed me of the little boy from Wainwright's that Heather was associating with.

At this I grew enraged. She was a pupil of mine and she was not to be enjoying the company of boys. I was incensed now at the very sight of the girl. How could a young lady of my teaching think it perfectly acceptable to meet with a boy in secret? I saw it as a personal insult. I had been putting a great deal of my energy into making that girl listen to me and follow the Bible as she was supposed to. Yet here she was gallivanting with a boy!

I will tell you right now, that could not go unpunished. The problem that I had was Mrs McGinley's attack of conscience. You see, she discovered her daughter's inappropriate friendship from reading her, that is Heather's, diary. I did not see that this was a problem as reading the diary managed to divert a disaster and stop the two seeing each other, or so we thought. I had to be subtle with Heather.

I punished her for her meetings with Jacob. I did not say that is what they were for but she knew she was wrong to see him so she must have expected to be punished. I only wish now that I had punished her more fervently. Now that I know she continued to see that boy after her mother had strictly forbade her from going anywhere near him.

My punishments did grow more intense. But with good reason. You see, one morning I received a letter from Mrs. McGinley requesting that I do whatever necessary to discipline her daughter. She had at last, to my great relief, given up on patience and subtly. She wanted her daughter to be chastised for her impertinence. They had grown tired of her insolence at home too you see. She was a very difficult child to deal with. I took great pleasure in helping this poor couple to come to terms with their insubordinate daughter.

Fern inhaled sharply. Heather's mother had actually asked Sister Ruth to punish her daughter continuously? That was beyond Fern's comprehension. She thought about her sons. They were mischievous at home and at school and she punished them when they were bad but never to this extent. She is prepared to take away pocket money and take away their privileges like the TVs they have in their rooms but she would never allow anyone to lock them in basements or leave them cold and alone at the bottom of a well. The incredulity of this moment took away any sadness. Fern was angry at Ruth, but now she was angry at Heather's mother as well. How can a mother be that irresponsible? How could a mother allow someone to abuse her child? Fern continued to read the dialogue.

What a lot of people do not understand about me is that I take pleasure in the disciplining of children. I am acting with righteousness and I am satisfied with the results. When a child is disobedient, I do what I deem necessary to make them obedient. That is the nature of my job.

I believe that we may be approaching the reason

145

that I am here. You see, I do not feel very guilty about the death of Heather. She deserved it in so many ways. If she had lived, she would have only caused more trouble. Every second God granted her, she used for mischief. However, the part of this story that eats away at me, the aspect of this tale that makes me ask questions is when I remember how I felt when I was punishing Heather. I was only able to do it because I had cause, and because God placed me on this earth to point young people in His direction.

The problem that I face, however, is not whether or not I was justified in how far I took the punishments. The problem that I have is that I enjoyed what I did. I liked to cause Heather pain. She was just a girl, like all the others. When I punished other girls I felt only boredom at the monotony of it all. With Heather it was different. It was as if she made me enjoy what I did to her. When I raised my cane above my head I felt the heat of anticipation burning inside me. The fear on her face made me smile. But the real pleasure came when the cane hit her. The feeling I got when the wood connected with her flesh was incredible. The sound of her squeal at the pain was enough to make me want to squeal with delight. I was always left with the desire to do it again. It thrilled me. I felt a sensation that I had never felt before. My stomach would tense up and my chest would tingle. When I hit her it all stopped and I just felt blissful. As my cane left her flesh the sensation began again. I felt alive when I hit her, I felt as if I would explode. My heart raced when I did it. I could see her recoil, but it merely urged me to continue. I do not understand why it is I enjoyed causing Heather such intense pain.

I began to hate her more and more. She was making me sin I knew she was and I was spending hours more than was necessary praying for forgiveness. One day I asked her to count the bricks on the inside of the well she eventually drowned in. Although on this day it was very shallow. She was such a silly girl. She fell in and ended up soaking wet from top to toe. When I saw her down there I knew she was in pain. I could see that she was desperate to get out but I did not want her to leave that place. I wanted her to stay down there forever. I wanted her to sit down there in agony, all day and all night until she died of the cold and the wet.

Then I would watch as her cheeks withdrew into her skull and her flesh began to recede as she started to rot. I would watch as the fidgety little pain in my side turns slowly into no more than bones. In actual fact, she stayed there just the rest of the day. I believe the caretaker lifted her out eventually. I experienced the most enjoyable afternoon of my teaching career that day. Not only was Heather not there, she was stuck somewhere dark. She was in pain and I knew that I could stop it. Only, I did not want to. I sat in my chair teaching the other girls with a slight smile on my face, as I basked in the delight of knowing what Heather was experiencing. Revelling in the fantasy that she may never get out.

But sitting just next to that satisfaction was a nagging feeling. I was glad she was not there, filling my classroom with ungodly sin. But I missed the punishments. I ached for the chance to raise that cane high above her exposed skin and bring it cracking down. Seeing the welt appear almost instantly. The cry of pain. The tears falling from her eyes and making my leg wet. I tried to push that nagging feeling away, tried to stop it from creeping into my thoughts but it would not cease. I found myself growing angry at the girl when she wasn't even here.

I don't know what it was that made me think of the basement. Students of the school were not allowed to go down there because the door could not be opened from the inside. I decided that whenever I could I would lock her in there. She deserved it for making me sin. For bringing sin into my classroom.

When I did send her down there it was almost as if I was in Heaven. The thought of her fear and her torment, in that cold, dark prison I had sent her to, was joyous beyond description. That day I was happier than I have ever been in my entire life. I did not punish a single other girl that day. In fact, I was asked if I was feeling well as I was teaching with a smile on my face. Smiles are hard to come by in the teaching profession. I wish I could go back and do it all over again. I would not do it differently. I would just do more of the same. I would have found new ways in which to punish Heather. I would have found new ways to find pleasure for myself.

Fern stood up,

"What a bitch!" She could not help it coming out of her mouth. She had sat and read Sister Ruth claiming to be a servant of God and now she was reading about Ruth being almost orgasmic at the idea that Heather was in pain. It was too much. Fern threw one of the folders at the wall so hard that it split open and the papers inside spilled onto the floor. The satisfaction she gained from this outburst was so great she was soon picking up more and more folders to throw at the wall.

This felt good, Fern had so much anger inside her, it needed releasing. Folder after folder was flung at the wall, each one harder than the last. Fern felt a little anger being purged as the sound of the folders hitting the wall and breaking filled her ears. After emptying the desk of most of its contents, she sat back down. There was still more to be read.

That is why I am here. I cannot work it out in my mind why I would feel like that. When I thought Heather had died in an accident I did not think anything of it. She was merely a stupid little girl who had strayed too close to a deep well. However, I discovered later that she had in fact taken her own life. This was the exact time that I began to slip in to a terrible confusion. You see, I was glad that she had killed herself. I was glad that she was dead and she had blamed me for it. It was when I thought about how awful these thoughts were that I started to do things that I'm told were a little unusual. I began to copy Heather's diary. I was desperate to understand why I felt so happy when she was in pain.

As I wrote her words I tried to imagine how she was feeling when she had written them. I put myself in her position. I closed my eyes to see the darkness, to understand the confusion she must have felt in the coal hut, the basement and the well. I searched my house for spiders to see if I could recreate her experience in the basement.

I looked at myself and tried to hate my reflection. All my efforts were in vain. You see it is hard to hate yourself when you believe the thing you are supposed to hate yourself for was right. I tried as hard as I could, but I just grew more and more blissful at the thought of her pain. I cannot understand why I felt like that. Why I still feel like that. I am a good person. I follow the bible. I am not supposed to gain pleasure from the pain of a fellow human. I still do not understand why I smile at the thought of Heather's agony. She was one of God's creations, however evil she was, I was still supposed to find love for her. But

149

it was impossible. I loved the feeling I got when I hurt her too much to try hard to love her instead.

Of course, this all made me hate Heather even more. I began to fear God's reaction to what I was feeling. The reason that I attacked Sister Mary and those policemen was because they were not sent to help me. They were sent to punish me. God sent them to punish me. It seems to me that they achieved their purpose. I am here now. I am being punished. I have been sent here because God sees fit to show me the repercussions of what I did to Heather. I abused His trust. He put His faith in me to restore Heather's soul and make her clean and good but I took advantage of that power and it made God angry. I am sorry of course but I have been sent to a place where, along with prayer, I can find the way back to God. I see also that I was sent here to guide others to His path alongside me. When I leave here I will have paid my price. I no longer fear for my soul.

Fern was amazed. She had images in her mind of Ruth being an incomprehensible mess from what Morgan told her. But Sister Ruth was mostly coherent from what she had read. Fern thought about the content of Ruth's letters. She was delusional and from what Fern knew, as well as what she had read, she was a danger as well.

Fern got up and busied herself tidying the papers away into the files. She had caused an awful mess but found the sorting to be therapeutic. She considered what she had read as she placed the papers back into their files. When she finished she left the room and walked down the corridor.

She was met with a big smile from the admin lady who had left her with the files.

"All finished?"

"Yes, thank you."

"Are you ok, Mrs Calvern?"

Fern looked up to meet the gaze of the concerned person who had given her something with no idea of the consequences.

"I learned a long time ago about the woman in this file but I had never read anything from her point of view. She was a bad person and I don't say that about a lot of people. She was bad and should never have been near children."

She handed the files back and walked away hoping she would not see the inside of this hospital for quite some time.

The images in her mind of Ruth enjoying the punishments. Of wanting to hurt Heather were too much. Tears stung her eyes. Her grief for Heather had been so real twenty years ago and now it was all back, renewed at the words of her tormenter. Full tears came as she thought of that young girl being tortured until she saw no way out other than ending her own life. It was a tragedy beyond anything else Fern had ever known.

She felt like a student again, she felt alone again. Fern needed to get home, to remind herself there was some comfort for her.

Chapter Nine

Fern walked back into her house and saw it differently. Everything seems a little brighter than normal, like someone had added more colour into the rooms. Her entire world had been turned upside down by the files at the hospital. She had thought that it was all over, that this had all finished long ago. She felt as though all the energy had been drained out of her. As if she could no longer think straight. There were too many thoughts in her mind all at once. It was hard for Fern to organise them. She had discovered so much more over the last few weeks and she knew what she should do next. She knew what Heather had wanted to do. Fern must write all this down. Properly this time, as a book. There was just one thing that Fern needed to do before she started. There was one question that she still needed answering. The question that had first raised itself in Fern's mind when Jacob's daughter had first come to visit. Why hadn't Morgan told her about Jacob's other diary. He must have known, he had spoken to Jacob's daughter all those years ago. She must have told Morgan about it.

Fern found some old address books and rummaged through them until she found the one with Morgan's number scribbled inside. He had given her his home phone number in case she needed it. She picked up the phone and called the man who had given her Heather McGinley's diary all those years ago.

He sounded much older now. He had retired from the university a long time ago and had dedicated his time since to doing research for local history essays he still wrote from time to time. She told Morgan everything, even her plans to write Heather's story, and asked him why he hadn't told her about the other diary.

"I don't understand Fern. You are telling me that Heather Rowland. Jacob's one and only daughter came to your house yesterday and gave you her father's diary?"

Fern had explained to Morgan what was inside and everything about the hospital. She didn't understand what was confusing him.

"Jacob's daughter can't have come to you, Fern. None of this makes any sense. Are you sure that is who she was?"

Fern was irritated with Morgan. Why didn't he believe her? Was he so proud that he could not accept that information was given to her and not him? That she had managed to find out more than he had without any help from him?

"Why are you so confused by this, Morgan? Heather came to this house and gave me that diary. I don't understand why you find it so hard to believe."

Morgan went quiet, Fern could hear him breathing down the phone, rasping slightly as he did so.

"I find it hard to believe that Heather Rowland gave you that diary, Fern because Heather Rowland has been dead for twenty years. She died the night I visited your flat and told you about the diary of her father's that I had read."

Fern felt as if she was sinking. She felt the blood drain from her face. She was still holding the phone but if Morgan was speaking she couldn't hear it. Heather was dead? But she had been in that house. She had sat directly opposite where she was sitting now. She had spoken to her. She had given Fern the address of the asylum. How was any of this possible? How could she have got that diary if Jacob's daughter was dead? Apparently she had said this last thought out loud and it was Morgan's response to it that snapped Fern back to reality.

"I don't know how you got it Fern but listen to me. Do you know what the date is today? It's the twelfth of October, the anniversary of Heather McGinley's death. Maybe you should think about taking a holiday or something. Rest for a while."

"What? Why do think I need a rest? Oh my God, you think I'm crazy don't you? You think that I imagined the whole thing. What, do you think that I just hallucinated this woman? Well, answer me this Morgan, if Jacob's daughter was a figment of my imagination then how come I have the diary? How come I got the address for the asylum? They didn't just appear magically."

"I don't think you are crazy, Fern. I just think that you need to take a time out. You have had a lot to deal with. Remember last time you got into this story too deep?"

Fern reached to her face and felt the scar that Sister Ruth had given her twenty years ago. She understood. Morgan believed her but he was concerned. He did not want her to get hurt again. She smiled. The smile soon turned into a laugh as she realised how ridiculous all this was. It was the kind of senseless laughter that occurs at a funeral or a hospital when you just can't think of any other way of dealing with something as emotional as a death or illness of a loved one. It was the kind of laughter that saves you from tears.

"You know, Fern, it is going to be very difficult to do. I tried to write about the history of Saint Agnes's almost forty years ago now. It was Heather's story that stopped me. But it was my research into that school that allowed you to discover all this information. I hope you do it, I want you to do it, and I always have. I think if there is one person in this world who deserves to be written about it is that tragic little girl. I know you can tell this story so that people will read it but I want you to be aware before you start something you most likely already know. This story touched you, whether or not your book will touch others remains to be seen but whatever the outcome the journey you are going to take in writing, this book is going to open up a lot of scars." She touched her cheek. "Emotional ones."

Fern lowered her hand and placed it on her chest. She understood the price of what she was about to do. But she also understood the value. Morgan was saying his goodbyes but his last words to Fern were both encouraging and kind.

"Be sure to send me a first edition."

Fern smiled wide. She felt like a young student again. She promised she would and hung up the phone. She walked into her living room and saw an old tatty book on her coffee table. She knew what it was. She had read it before. But not since. She picked up Heather's diary and opened it to the first page. All the memories came flooding back to her. The innocent hope of the opening entry, then the swift fall into depression. All Fern's thoughts and feelings about Heather came back. She realised as she sat and read the diary from cover to cover, finding out things that she not previously known, the entries she had missed when Heather's ghost had turned the pages for her. As Fern read the new information she understood the deep friendship that had existed between Heather and Jacob. With this understanding came also the understanding of why it was so important to tell this story. After one of Jacob's severe lashings from his father, he had run to Heather. When she saw the wounds he had and the pain that he was in she wept. She could not stand to see him in pain and she dressed the wounds with so much care that Jacob felt no extra pain as she bound his skin with bandages.

She wrote so vividly about this event that Fern was unable to stop herself from crying. She read on through the tears. She learnt that Sister Ruth had caught Heather and Jacob playing on Holly Street one day and had made sure that they were both severely punished. They were both made to scrub the floors of their own classroom until their hands bled. The stories seemed endless, Fern felt that she had understood Heather's pain before but she was not even close. She was tortured by Sister Ruth almost every single day she spent with that woman. Ruth would make Heather recite poems she did not know and do sums she did not understand. Heather was the only girl in her class who was forced to suffer this. Fern understood more and more the need for this story to be told. She understood that Morgan wanted it

155

as much as Heather did. That is why he left the diary with Fern. He knew that she had not read all of it and he knew that if she did, she would understand why she had to do it. He was right, Fern knew that the story of Heather McGinley must be told.

Fern turned the diary over in her hands. She looked at it with affection. How could she not have realised this all before? This story had made her laugh and cry and grow angry. She had felt pain and joy and disgust. All of this makes a story worth telling, and at the heart of it all, a little girl who taught Fern so much about her own ambition through the loss of freedom and life. Now that she had the whole story there were no more excuses. Fern walked out of the living room and down the hall into the kitchen. She was so happy. It was as if she had just found out what her life's purpose was. If she only wrote one more book, it would be to tell Heather's story.

Fern walked into the study and looked at her husband. He was writing notes on a pad of paper next to the phone. He had clearly had a stressful day, there was a small pile of sweet wrappers on the table next to his notebook. He stopped writing and he saw his wife looking at him with a strange look of serenity mixed with determination on her face.

"Are you alright?"

But his question had to wait. Ann had just walked through the door with Edward and Michael in tow.

"You will never believe the trouble this one has been in today."

She was pointing at Michael. Fern could well believe the trouble he had been in. It was only every once in a while that Michael came home after being good all day. "He took another student's football without asking at lunchtime and after he got bored playing with it he kicked it clean over the wall. One of the teachers had to go and fetch the ball from some poor old lady's garden."

"I didn't take it without asking, mum. It was one of the school's balls and he had finished with it. I didn't mean to kick it over the wall honest. The only reason James said I took it is because he doesn't like me."

Fern looked at Andrew who always seemed to be stifling a giggle at the antics of his sons and often proved to be no use at all at disciplining the boys for what they had done at school. However, Andrew's bad day had clearly taken its toll and he was looking rather fearsome. Fern left him to it as he demanded to know exactly what had happened.

Fern turned to look at Edward. He was a lot more timid than his brother and had not uttered a single word since he had come through the door. He was clutching a piece of paper in his arms. Fern allowed her curiosity to get the better of her. Edward always did so well at school but he did so quietly. She wanted to see what he had done this time to make her proud. Fern ushered him out of the kitchen and into the hall. They stood next to a window, on the shelf beneath it was the professional family photograph they had had taken last year. Edward had a cast on his arm after he had fallen down a set of steps the week before.

"What's that you have Edward?"

"It's nothing, mum. Just something I did at school."

"Well, can I see it?"

Edward was apprehensive. He was clutching the paper closer to him than before. It was evident that he did not want his mother to see it. The problem Edward had was that Fern wanted to look at that piece of paper. He had learned a long time ago that his mother always ended up getting what she wanted. He gave in.

"I suppose so."

Fern took the paper firmly from her son and looked at it. A smile grew across her face as she read what was written on it.

"Why didn't you want me to see this Ed? This is fantastic."

"I knew you'd make a big deal out of it. I didn't want you to go, you know, over the top."

"Over the top?!"

Fern suddenly realised what he meant by this when her reaction made Edward jump. She lowered herself down so that she was eye to eye with her son.

"This is nothing to be ashamed of. When you do things like this you should be shouting it from the rooftops not hiding it from your family."

"I know, I'm sorry."

A thought suddenly occurred to Fern,

"Edward, are there any more of these that you have been hiding from me?"

Edward tilted his eyes sheepishly up towards his mother. She knew that he had as soon as their eyes met. She pointed upstairs and Edward knew what his mother meant. He led her silently up to his room. Fern stood at the door and watched as Edward scrambled beneath his bed. He spent a few moments moving things around and mumbling the odd word that sounded as if they might be rude. Under normal circumstances, Fern would have gone scolded him for swearing but she let it go this time. There was something much more important going on.

Eventually he emerged holding a large box full of paper. Fern's eyes grew wide, she took the box and began to read the stories that her son had been writing for who knows how long. They were full of spelling mistakes and the grammar left a lot to be desired but the tales were wonderful. There were stories of pirates sailing around the world in search of treasure, tales of pixies and elves. Stories about lions and sharks and a whole host of fantastical creatures he had invented himself. He had such a vivid imagination. Fern must have sat there for half an hour before she realised that Edward was still standing and watching her.

"These are really good, Ed. Really good. I didn't know

you wrote stories. Why didn't you tell me? You know how happy it would have made me?"

"I just didn't want to disappoint you. You are so good at stories and I didn't want you to read anything I had written until they were as good as yours."

Fern smiled wider than she ever had done, pride and heartbreak mixing together inside her. She stood up and took Edward in her arms. What an amazing boy she thought as she squeezed him tightly. She hugged him so tightly in fact that he had to ask her to stop because he couldn't breathe.

"These stories are fantastic, Edward. Just one piece of advice I want to give you. Whenever you write a story, let me read it, eh?"

Edward smiled now and he promised his mother that he would let her read his stories. They left his bedroom and went downstairs. Fern was so pleased with her child. What made it all the more wonderful was that she could be his mentor. She would look forward to reading whatever he wrote next. She was so pleased that she had found this out. She shared something with Edward now that ran deep. She had written stories as a child. Mostly they were about horses because she had wanted one and the only way she could have one was to write about them. She understood that her son would be using his stories in a similar way. And that understanding was very special indeed. Fern entered the kitchen having almost forgotten what had happened to her that day.

With the kids tucked safely up in bed and Ann sent home for the day, at least a dozen mumblings about Michael and how a bit of discipline wouldn't do him any harm, Fern and Andrew sat and watched TV in peace. It was the time of the day that usually passed wordlessly.   Tonight was different however. Both were welcoming the end of a very long hard day but the pair were restless. Andrew was turning Michael over in his mind, wondering how to tackle his ill-behaved son. And Fern had something else on her mind. The brief respite that Edward's stories had provided had given way and been replaced by a growing concern. Fern knew she had to tell Andrew about her day. It had been one of the strangest and, in a way, one of the most exciting days of her life. She picked up the remote control and pushed the standby button.

"Hey, I was watching that you big bully!"

Fern ignored her husband's protest. He was still irritated from his busy day and Michael's behaviour.

"I know what my next book is going to be."

"Yeah, I know. The thing about the talking lions." Andrew said without even thinking anything of it. "I've been thinking about that, Fern and don't you think the message should be about responsibility or something? I think a lot of kids are too young for feminism."

"Very funny Andrew but that isn't what I meant. I'm not doing the lion thing. I mean I can't do it. The point is the lion story wasn't my idea. I heard it a long time ago from a little girl and I forgot that it was her idea and not mine."

"So what are you going to do instead? Still want to do a book for children?"

"No, I have a better story. But I need you to listen carefully to me because I have a lot I need to tell you. It's quite difficult for me to explain so please bear with me, ok?"

Andrew nodded and Fern described the day's events to her husband. Everything from the first visit from Heather all the way through to Edward's stories. By the time she had finished she felt relieved to have got all of it off her chest but Andrew looked a little perplexed.

"A dead woman came to our house and gave you a diary?"

"Yes."

"You went to a hospital and read the files of a schizophrenic nun?"

"Yes."

"And our son has been writing stories all his life and hidden them from you because he had a complex about not living up to the bestselling author he has for a mother?"

"Yes."

The couple stared at each other for a second and then, much to Fern's annoyance, Andrew burst out laughing.

"This is it, Fern. You have really lost it this time. I think we need to take you back to that mental health ward and see if they will take you in!"

Fern stood up from the sofa, filled with rage and defiance.

"Oh, well. Thank you very much Mr. Supportive! This is really important to me, Andrew. I've told you about Heather before and you said that you believed me. You said that you were prepared to have an open mind about something that I believed so strongly in. Why can't you do that again? I knew you would do this, I knew you would take the magic out of this story. You always do, you have no imagination! Why can't you, just for once, look outside the little safety net you call science and believe that there can be something else? Something outside of logical explanation. Just because you can't prove something does not mean that it is impossible. Yes, a woman who was supposed to have died twenty years ago turned up on my doorstep today and gave me her father's diary. And yes I went to a hospital to read Sister Ruth's files. I drove a long way to read the comments of a truly evil woman. I feel dirty just thinking about the things she said in that place. I really went on a roller coaster in there today.

And yes, the dead lady came back and she asked me to write a book about Heather McGinley. And I am going to; I have every intention of doing what she asked. Not because she wants me to, I'm not doing it for her; she just needed to give me a push in the right direction. That is what she did. Figment of my over active imagination or not, she gave me what I needed and now I can do something I have wanted to do for years."

Fern sat down in an arm chair opposite her husband. She was drained. Physically and mentally drained. This whole day had been a nightmare. The last thing she wanted to endure was a condescending analysis of her mental state from her husband. Andrew came over to Fern and put his arm around her.

"I'm sorry. I do believe you. I swear I believe you. I would not have stayed married to you if I couldn't cope with a little magic here and there. That is why I love you, Fern. Because you make everything magical."

Fern looked up and saw tears welling at the edges of her husband's eyes, waiting for one more drop to push them over the side and come rolling down his face. She loved him so much. A smile crept back onto Fern and then Andrew's face.

"I asked you before; right when we were first married why you hadn't written it yet. I'll admit I've thought about it now and then. Especially when you have a book published. The story had such an amazing effect on you. I guess you just weren't ready."

"It's not that. I have more information now, things I didn't even know about when I was a student. I can give the whole account now. I can tell all the sides of the story. Let people make their own minds up. All I want people to know is that Heather was a girl who died because she was not able to be the person she had dreamed of becoming. If I achieve nothing else I want to get that across. Maybe I could even prevent it from happening again.

"She touched my life, Andrew. She changed me. If you had met me before all this happened you would have found me to be quite different. Heather gave me ambition and desire to fulfil my dreams. I feel as if she is living through me now. Whenever I stop and think that all this writing is getting too much and I day dream about packing it all in I think about Heather. Her face comes back to me. Not her happy smiling face but her dead face. The face that I saw down the well in my dreams. She will always be inside me because I can never forget her. I won't allow myself to forget her."

Fern put her hand to her face. She felt the scar that ran down her cheek. It had faded well over the years and she did not even notice it when she looked in the mirror anymore. But it was still there, and feeling at it now made her remember that terrifying night when she got it.

"I'm not allowed to forget her."

Andrew looked at his wife. He had just taken a leap of faith. Everything he had built his career on had to be ignored if he was to believe his wife. As he took his exhausted wife to bed they were both lost in deep contemplation. They had a great deal to consider, they had both begun their next projects at the same time. This meant that they would not get any more peace for a while. Fern lay in bed and fell asleep thinking about how she would start Heather's story.

Fern sat down at her laptop and took in a deep breath. She glanced down briefly at the plan she had made for this book and the scribbled account she had written twenty years ago that she had kept safe and hidden. It was the most important thing she had ever written and she had to make sure that it was right. Fern allowed her mind to wander for a brief minute. She went back over the entire story. The school came back into her vision and words floated around in her mind as she tried to think of the best way to describe it. Heather and Jacob's friendship drifted in and out of her mind. The only thing she did not have trouble remembering was Sister Ruth's face. She had seen it in her dreams and in that picture at the asylum. A long list of negative words announced themselves as appropriate to describe the nun. Then the fear of that face she had seen that night in her mirror. She had blamed it on alcohol at the time. It had been a long time since she had believed that.

All the conversations she had with Erica about her

haunted flat seemed so stupid to Fern at the time. She wished that she could speak to Erica again and tell her she was right. She wondered if Erica would even believe what Fern had to say about the ghosts of Heather and Ruth. With difficulty Fern recalled the dreams. They had made so little sense at the time but now everything was so clear. She thought about the night she had released Heather, about how she had sat for hours, exhausted at her efforts to expel the spirit of Sister Ruth from her home. She was trying to think when it had started. She had written an intensive timeline but she didn't think that the story really began when Heather was at school. Not her story anyway. Fern felt the story had to start with her. That is what she knew. She knew about moving in to that flat and how it felt to experience those things all by herself and discover this story piece by piece over so many years. She opened a file and began with the line;

It was fantastic. Everything that she had wanted.

Acknowledgements

Writing a book is a weird experience. Something I've always wanted to achieve but I wandered in unprepared. The first draft of this book was completed when I was 20 years old (2003) in the gap between year 2 and 3 of university, and I was told by a university lecturer that no one could write a book in 2 months. She was right, of course, although I took the comment to heart and shelved the book for 20 years.

Coming back to it I got to meet myself at 20 and there were certain parts of the book that screamed naivety. But thanks to my sister, who happens to be an expert in mental health and mental health facilities, I was able to add some authenticity into the book.

My husband was also an immeasurable help, his knowledge of educational institutions gave credence to the school scenes.

They both helped edit and, those who have done this will know, it took a long time. So, 21 years later Heather is finally a real, physical thing that I, and you, can hold and enjoy. It still seems like a dream.

I do hope you enjoy this; it has been a labour of love and to have people read and enjoy it would be the icing on the cake. Stay spooky.

Full of Rot and Poetry
Rotten Poetry

RottenPoetry.net
@RottenPoetryEmporium

Creative community, incredible events, love of literature.

Literature blog, bookish gifts, literary t-shirts,
poetry, history, philosophy, art.

Visit us at:
RottenPoetry.net